PENGUIN BOOKS
A HANDFUL OF NUTS

Ruskin Bond's first novel, *The Room on the Roof*, written when he was seventeen, won the John Llewellyn Rhys Memorial Prize in 1957. Since then he has written several novellas (including *Vagrants in the Valley*, *A Flight of Pigeons* and *Delhi Is Not Far*), essays, poems and children's books, many of which have been published by Penguin India. He has also written over 500 short stories and articles that have appeared in a number of magazines and anthologies. He received the Sahitya Akademi Award in 1993 and the Padma Shri in 1999.

Ruskin Bond was born in Kasauli, Himachal Pradesh, and grew up in Jamnagar, Dehradun, Delhi and Shimla. As a young man, he spent four years in the Channel Islands and London. He returned to India in 1955 and has never left the country since. He now lives in Landour, Mussoorie, with his adopted family.

ALSO BY RUSKIN BOND

Fiction
The Room on the Roof & Vagrants in the Valley
The Night Train at Deoli and Other Stories
Time Stops at Shamli and Other Stories
Our Trees Still Grow in Dehra
A Season of Ghosts
When Darkness Falls and Other Stories
A Flight of Pigeons
Delhi Is Not Far
A Face in the Dark and Other Hauntings
The Sensualist
A Handful of Nuts

Non-fiction
Rain in the Mountains
Scenes from a Writer's Life
The Lamp Is Lit
The Little Book of Comfort
Landour Days
Notes from a Small Room

Anthologies
Dust on the Mountain: Collected Stories
The Best of Ruskin Bond
Friends in Small Places
Indian Ghost Stories (ed.)
Indian Railway Stories (ed.)
Classical Indian Love Stories and Lyrics (ed.)
Tales of the Open Road
Ruskin Bond's Book of Nature
Ruskin Bond's Book of Humour
A Town Called Dehra

Poetry
Ruskin Bond's Book of Verse

A Handful of Nuts

RUSKIN BOND

PENGUIN BOOKS

An imprint of Penguin Random House

PENGUIN BOOKS

USA | Canada | UK | Ireland | Australia
New Zealand | India | South Africa | China | Singapore

Penguin Books is part of the Penguin Random House group of companies
whose addresses can be found at global.penguinrandomhouse.com

Published by Penguin Random House India Pvt. Ltd
4th Floor, Capital Tower 1, MG Road,
Gurugram 122 002, Haryana, India

Penguin
Random House
India

Published as part of Strangers in the Night: Two Novellas 1996
This edition first published by Penguin Books India 2009

ISBN 9780143067405

Typeset in Goudy Old Style CGATT by SÜRYA, New Delhi

Printed at Manipal Technologies Limited, India

www.penguin.co.in

MIX
Paper | Supporting
responsible forestry
FSC® C043100

This is a legitimate digitally printed version of the book and therefore might not
have certain extra finishing on the cover.

Author's Note

Although written when I was sixty, A *Handful of Nuts* is about myself at twenty-one, an age that is important to each one of us. It is an age at which we have to come to terms with our own natures if we are to survive the rigours of life's long journey to the end of our chosen road.

Twenty-one was a year of special significance for me. I had published by first book; I was full of hope and ambition, prepared to take chances; and I saw myself as a great lover, as indeed most of us do at that age. I now believe that great lovers are born, not made.

As I grow older, life seems to grow more comical, and I find myself better suited to playing the clown than the romantic hero. At twenty-one, we all aspire to be romantic heroes (or heroines), often with disastrous results. It's an awkward age. You need either money or a beautiful figure to get away with it, and I had neither.

I wrote *A Handful of Nuts* over a period of three-and-a-half months one winter, when icy winds and occasional snowstorms kept me confined to my small abode in the hills. I felt a longing for the hot, languorous summer days of my youth, and in this short novel I tried to recapture something of that time and place. Please do not take it as straight autobiography. Some of the people, places and incidents were real; others, creatures of my imagination. It is said that a good story-teller is someone who has a good memory and hopes that other people haven't! I don't think my memory is better than anyone else's, but it is selective, as a writer's must be, and if I have neglected to include some important friends in this novella it is only because I have saved them up for another tale.

A Handful of Nuts is a novella, a form that seems to suit my style and temperament. Only the French (and occasionally the Americans) have really done justice to the short novel. The British prefer the proliferation of the longer novel, and British publishers won't look at a novella; they want their money's worth of words. But the short novel, with its compositional economy and homogeneity of conception, has its place in the scheme of things, as Conrad demonstrated in *Heart of Darkness*, *The Shadow-Line*, *Youth* and *The Nigger of Narcissus*. But he was a Pole writing in English.

In *A Handful of Nuts* I am my usual irreverent self; it is a self-portrait of the author as a sensitive and occasionally mischievous youth. Or rather, of a mischievous elderly author looking back on his innocent youth! If the story has a literary ancestor, it would be Sterne's *Sentimental Journey*.

Landour   RUSKIN BOND

March 2009

One

It wasn't the room on the roof, but it was a large room with a balcony in front and a small verandah at the back. On the first floor of an old shopping complex, still known as Astley Hall, it faced the town's main road, although a walled-in driveway separated it from the street pavement. A neem tree grew in front of the building, and during the early rains, when the neem-pods fell and were crushed underfoot, they gave off a rich, pungent odour which I can never forget.

I had taken the room at the very modest rent of thirty-five rupees a month, payable in advance to the stout Punjabi widow who ran the provisions store downstairs. Her provisions ran to rice, lentils, spices and condiments, but I wasn't doing any cooking then, there wasn't time, so for a quick snack I'd cross the road and consume a couple of samosas or vegetable patties. Whenever I received a decent fee for a story, I'd treat myself to some sliced ham and a loaf of bread, and make myself ham sandwiches. If any of my friends were around, like Jai Shankar or William Matheson, they'd make short work of the ham sandwiches.

I don't think I ever went hungry, but I was certainly underweight and and undernourished, eating irregularly in cheap restaurants and dhabas and suffering frequent stomach upheavals. My four years in England had done nothing to improve my constitution, as there, too, I had lived largely on what was sold over the counter in snack-bars—baked beans on toast being the standard fare.

At the corner of the block, near the Orient Cinema, was a little restaurant called Komal's, run by a rotund Sikh gentleman who seldom left his seat near the window. Here I had a reasonably good lunch of dal, rice and a vegetable curry, for two or three rupees.

There were a few other regulars—a college teacher, a couple of salesmen and occasionally someone waiting for a film show to begin. William and Jai did not trail me to this place, as it was a little lowbrow for them (William being Swiss and Jai being Doon School); nor was it frequented much by students or children. It was lower middle-class, really; professional men who were still single and forced to eat in the town. I wasn't bothered by anyone here. And it suited me in other ways, because there was a news-stand close by and I could buy a paper or a magazine and skim through it before or after my meal. Determined as I was to making a living by writing, I had made it my duty to study every English language publication that found its way to Dehra (most of them did), to see which of them published short fiction. A surprisingly large number of magazines did publish short stories; the trouble was, the rates of payment were not very high, the average being about twenty-five rupees a story.

Ten stories a month would therefore fetch me two hundred and fifty rupees—just enough for me to get by!

After eating at Komal's, I made my way to the up-market Indiana for a cup of coffee, which was all I could afford there. Indiana was for the smart set. In the evenings it boasted a three-piece band, and you could dance if you had a partner, although dancing cheek to cheek went out with World War Two. From noon to three, Larry Gomes, a Dehra boy of Goan origin, tinkled on the piano, playing old favourites or new hits.

That spring morning, only one or two tables were occupied—by business people, who weren't listening to music—so Larry went through a couple of old numbers for my benefit, *September Song* and *I'll See You Again*. At twenty, I was very old-fashioned. Larry received three hundred rupees a month and a free lunch, so he was slightly better off than me. Also, his father owned a small music and record shop a short distance away.

While I was sipping my coffee and pondering upon my financial affairs (which were non-existent, as I had no finances), in walked the rich and baggy-eyed Maharani of Magador with her daughter Indu. I stood up to greet her and she gave me a gracious smile.

She knew that some five years previously, when I was in my last year at school, I had been infatuated with her daughter. She had even intercepted one of my love letters, but she had been quite sporting about it, and had told me that I wrote a nice letter. Now she knew that I was writing stories for magazines, and she said, 'We read your story in the *Weekly* last week. It was quite charming, didn't I say you'd make a good writer?' I blushed and thanked her, while Indu gave me a mischievous smile. She was still at college.

'You must come and see us someday,' said the Maharani and moved on majestically. Indu, small-boned and petite and dressed in something blue, looked more than ever like a butterfly; soft, delicate, flitting away just. as you thought you could touch her.

They sat at a table in a corner, and I returned to my contemplation of the coffee-stains on the table-cloth. I had, of course, splashed my coffee all over the place.

Larry had observed my confusion, and guessing its cause, now played a very old tune which only Indu's mother would have recognized: 'I kiss your little bands, madame, I long to kiss your lips . . .'

On my way out, Larry caught my eye and winked at me. 'Next time I'll give you a tip,' I said.

'Save it for the waiter,' said Larry.

It was hot in the April sunshine, and I headed for my room, wishing I had a fan.

Stripping to vest and underwear, I lay down on the bed and stared at the ceiling. The ceiling stared back at me. I turned on my side and looked across the balcony, at the leaves of the neem tree. They were absolutely still. There. was not even the promise of a breeze.

I dozed off, and dreamt of my princess, her deep dark eyes and the tint of winter moonlight on her cheeks. I dreamt that I was bathing with her in a clear moonlit pool, while small fishes of gold and silver and mother-of-pearl slipped between our thighs. I laved her exquisite little body with the fresh spring water and placed a hibiscus flower between her golden breasts and another behind her ear. I was overcome with lust and threw myself upon her, only to discover that she had turned into a fish with silver scales.

I opened my eyes to find Sitaram, the washerman's son, sitting at the foot of my bed.

Sitaram must have been about sixteen, a skinny boy with large hands, large feet and large ears. He had loose sensual lips. An unprepossessing youth, whom I found irritating in the extreme; but as he lived with his parents in the quarters behind the flat, there was no avoiding him.

'How did you get in here?' I asked brusquely.

'The door was open.'

'That doesn't mean you can walk right in. What do you want?'

'Don't you have any clothes for washing? My father asked.'

'I wash my own clothes.'

'And sheets?' He studied the sheet I was lying on. 'Don't you wash your sheet? It is very dirty.'

'Well, it's the only one I've got. So buzz off.'

But he was already pulling the sheet out from under me. 'I'll wash it for you free. You are a nice man. My mother says you are *seeda-saada*, very innocent.'

'I am not innocent. And I need the sheet.'

'I will bring you another. I will lend it to you free. We get lots of sheets to wash. Yesterday six sheets came from the hospital. Some people were killed in a bus accident.'

'You mean the sheets came from the morgue— they were used to cover dead bodies? I don't want a sheet from the morgue.'

'But it is very clean. You know *khatmals* can't live on dead bodies. They like fresh blood.'

He went away with my sheet and came back five minutes later with a freshly-pressed bedsheet.

'Don't worry,' he said. 'It's not from the hospital.'

'Where is this one from?'

'Indiana Hotel. I will give them a hospital sheet in exchange.'

TWO

The gardens were bathed in moonlight, as I walked down the narrow old roads of Dehra—I stopped near the Maharani's house and looked over the low wall. The lights were still on in some of the rooms. I waited for some time until I saw Indu come to a window. She had a book in her hand, so I guessed she'd been reading. Maybe if I sent her a poem, she'd read it. A poem about a small red virgin rose.

But it wouldn't bring me any money.

I walked back to the bazaar, to the bright lights of the cinemas and small eating houses. It was only eight o'clock. The street was still crowded. Nowadays it's traffic; then it was just full of people. And so you were constantly bumping into people you knew—or did not know . . .

I was staring at a poster of Nimmi, sexiest of

Indian actresses, when a hand descended on my shoulder, and I turned to see Jai Shankar, the genius from the Doon School, whose father owned the New Empire Cinema.

'Jalebis, Ruskin, jalebis,' he crooned. Although he was from a rich family, he never seemed to have any pocket money. And of course it's easier to borrow from a poor man than it is to borrow from a rich one! Why is that, I wonder? There was William Matheson, for instance, who lived in a posh boarding-house, but was always cadging small sums off me—to pay his laundry bill or assist in his consumption of Charminar cigarettes: without them he was a nervous wreck. And with Jai Shankar it was jalebis . . .

'I haven't had a cheque for weeks,' I told him.

'What about the story you were writing for the BBC?'

'Well, I've just sent it to them.'

'And the novel you were writing?'

'I'm still writing it.'

'Jalebis will cost only two rupees.'

'Oh, all right . . .'

Jai Shankar stuffed himself with jalebis while I contented myself with a samosa. Jai wished to be an artist, poet and diarist, somewhat in the manner of Andre Gide, and had even given me a copy of Gide's *Fruits of the Earth* in an endeavour to influence me in the same direction. It is still with me today, forty years later, his spidery writing scrawling a message across the dancing angel drawn on the title-page. Our favourite books outlast our dreams . . .

Of course, after the jalebis I had to see Jai home. If I hadn't met him, someone else would have had to walk home with him. He was terrified of walking down the narrow lane to his house once darkness had fallen. There were no lights and the overhanging mango, neem and peepal trees made it a place of Stygian gloom. It was said that a woman had hanged herself from a mango tree on this very lane, and Jai was always in a dither lest he should see the lady dangling in front of him.

He kept a small pocket torch handy, but after leaving him at his gate I would have to return sans torch, for nothing could persuade him to part with it. On the way back, I would bump into other pedestrians who would be stumbling along the lane, guided by slivers of moonlight or the pale glimmer from someone's window.

Only the blind man carried a lamp.

'And what need have you of a light?' we asked.

'So that fools do not stumble against me in the dark.'

But I did not care for torchlight. I had taught myself to use whatever the night offered— moonlight, full and partial; starlight; the light from street lamps, from windows, from half-open doors. The night is beautiful, made ugly only by the searing headlights of cars.

When I got back to my room, the shops had closed and only the lights in Sitaram's quarters were on. His parents were quarrelling, and the entire neighbourhood could hear them. It was always like that. The husband was drunk and abusive; she refused to open the door for him, told him to go and sleep with a whore or, better still, a donkey. After some time he retreated into the dark.

I had no lights, as my landlady had neglected to pay the electricity bill for the past six months. But I did not mind the absence of light, although at times I would have liked an electric fan.

It meant, of course, that I could not type or even write by hand except when the full moon

poured over the balcony. But I could always
manage a few lines of poetry on a large white
sheet of paper.

This sheet of paper is my garden,
These words my flowers.
I do not ask a miracle this night,
Other than you beside me in the bright
   moonlight.
Naked, entwined like the flowering vine . . .

And there I got stuck. The last lines always
fox me, one reason why I shall never be a poet.

'And we cling to each other for a long, long
time . . .' Shades of *September Song*?

In any case, I couldn't send it to Indu, as her
mother would be sure to intercept the letter and
read it first. The idea of her daughter clinging to
me like a vine would not have appealed to the
Maharani.

I would have to think of a more mundane
method of making my feelings known.

Three

There was some excitement, as Stewart Granger, the British film actor, was in town.

Stewart Granger in Dehradun? Occasionally, a Bombay film star passed through, but this was the first time we were going to see a foreign star. We all knew what he looked like, of course. The Odeon and Orient cinemas had been showing British and American films since the days of the silent movies. Occasionally, they still showed 'silents', as their sound systems were antiquated and the projectors rattled a good deal, drowning the dialogue. This did not matter if the star was John Wayne (or even Stewart Granger) as their lines were quite predictable, but it made a difference if you were trying to listen to Nelson Eddy sing *At the Balalaika* or Hope and Crosby exchanging wisecracks.

We had assembled outside the Indiana and were discussing the phenomenon of having Stewart Granger in town. What was he doing here?

'Making a film, I suppose,' I ventured.

Suresh Mathur, the lawyer, demurred, 'What about? Nobody's written a book about Dehra, except you, Ruskin, and no one has read yours. Has someone bought the film rights?'

'No such luck. And besides, the hero is sixteen and Stewart Granger is thirty-six.'

'Doesn't matter. They'll change the story.'

'Not if I can help it.'

William Matheson had another theory.

'He's visiting his old aunt in Rajpur.'

'We never knew he had an aunt in Rajpur.'

'Nor did I. It's just a theory.'

'You and your theories. We'll ask the owner of Indiana. Stewart Granger is going to stay here, isn't he?'

Mr Kapoor of Indiana enlightened us. 'They're location-hunting for a shikar movie. It's called *Harry Black and the Tiger*.

'Stewart Granger is playing a black man?' asked William.

'No, no, that's an English surname.'

'English is a funny language,' said William,

who believed in the superiority of the French tongue.

'We don't have any tigers left in these forests,' I said.

'They'll bring in a circus tiger and let it loose,' said Suresh.

'In the jungle, I hope,' said William. 'Or will they let it loose on Rajpur Road?'

'Preferably in the Town Hall,' said Suresh, who was having some trouble with the municipality over his house tax.

Stewart Granger did not disappoint.

At about two in the afternoon, the hottest part of the day, he arrived in an open Ford convertible, shirtless and vestless. He was in his prime then, in pretty good condition after playing opposite Ava Gardner in *Bhowani Junction*, and everyone remarked on his fine torso and general good looks. He made himself comfortable in a cool corner of the Indiana and proceeded to down several bottles of chilled beer, much to everyone's admiration. Larry Gomes, at the piano, started playing *Sweet Rosie O'Grady* until Granger, who wasn't Irish, stopped him and asked for something more modern. Larry obliged with *Goodnight Irene*, and Stewart, now into his third bottle of beer, began singing the refrain. At the next table, William, Suresh and I, trying to keep pace with the star's consumption of beer, joined in the chorus, and before long there was a mad sing-song in the restaurant.

The editor of the local paper, *The Doon Chronicle*, tried interviewing the star, but made little progress. Someone gave him an information and publicity sheet which did the rounds. It said Stewart Granger was born in 1913, and that he had black hair and brown eyes. He still had them—unless the hair was a toupe. It said his height was 6 feet 2 inches, and that he weighed 196 lbs. He looked every pound of it. It also said his youthful ambition was to become a 'nerve specialist'. We looked at him with renewed respect, although none of us was quite sure what a 'nerve specialist' was supposed to do.

'We just get on your nerves,' said Mr Granger when asked, and everyone laughed.

He tucked into his curry and rice with relish, downed another beer and returned to his waiting car. A few good-natured jests, a wave and a smile, and the star and his entourage drove off into the foothills.

We heard, later, that they had decided to make the film in Mysore, in distant south India.

No wonder it turned out to be a flop. Sorry, Stewart.

Two months later, Yul Brynner passed through but he didn't cause the same excitement. We were getting used to film stars. His film wasn't made in Dehra, either. They did it in Spain. Another flop.

Four

Why have I chosen to write about the twenty-first year of my life?

Well, for one thing, it's often the most significant year in any young person's life. A time for falling in love; a time to set about making your dreams come true; a time to venture forth, to blaze new trails, take risks, do your own thing, follow your star ... And so it was with me.

I was just back after four years of living in the West; I had found a publisher in London for my first novel; I was looking for fresh fields and new laurels; and I wanted to prove that I could succeed as a writer with my small home town in India as a base, without having to live in London or Paris or New York.

In a couple of weeks' time it would be my twenty-first birthday, and I was feeling good about it.

I had mentioned the date to someone—Suresh Mathur, I think—and before long I was being told by everyone I knew that I would have to celebrate the event in a big way, twenty-one being an age of great significance in a young man's life. To tell the truth I wasn't feeling very youthful. Komal's rich food, swimming in oil, was beginning to take its toll, and I spent a lot of time turning input into output, so to speak.

Finding me flat on my back, Sitaram sat down beside me on my bed and expressed his concern for my health. I was too weak to drive him away.

'Just a stomach upset,' I said. 'It will pass off. You can go.'

'I will bring you some curds—very good for the stomach when you have the *dast*—when you are in full flow.'

'I took some tablets.'

'Medicine no good. Take curds.'

Seeing that he was serious, I gave him two rupees and he went off somewhere and returned after ten minutes with a bowl of curds. I found it quite refreshing, and he promised to bring more that evening. Then he said: 'So you will be twenty-one soon. A big party.'

'How did you know?' I asked, for I certainly hadn't mentioned it to him.

'Sitaram knows everything!'

'How did you find out?'

'I heard them talking in the Indiana, as I collected the table-cloths for washing. Will you have the party in Indiana?'

'No, no, I can't afford it.'

'Have it here then. I will help you.'

'Let's see . . .'

'How many people will you call for the tea-party?'

'I don't know. Most of them are demanding beer—it's expensive.'

'Give them *kachi*, they make it in our village behind the police lines. I'll bring a jerry-can for you. It's very cheap and very strong. Big *nasha!*'

'How do you know? Do you drink it?'

'I never drink. My father drinks enough for everyone.'

'Well, I can't give it to my guests.'

'Who will come?'

I gave some consideration to my potential guest list. There'd be Jai Shankar demanding jalebis and beer, a sickening combination! And William Matheson wanting French toast, I supposed. (Was French toast eaten by the French? It seemed very English, somehow.) And Suresh Mathur wanting something stronger than beer. (After two whiskeys, he claimed that he had discovered the fourth dimension.) And there were my young Sikh friends from the Dilaram Bazaar, who would be happy with lots to eat. And perhaps Larry Gomes would drop in.

Dare I invite the Maharani and Indu? Would they fit in with the rest of the mob? Perhaps I could invite them to a separate tea-party at the Indiana. Cream-rolls and cucumber sandwiches.

And where would the money come from for all these celebrations? My bank balance stood at a little over three hundred rupees—enough to pay the rent and the food bill at Komal's and make myself a new pair of trousers. The pair I'd bought on the Mile End Road in London, two years previously, were now very baggy and had a shine on the seat. The other pair, made of non-shrink material, got smaller at every wash. I had given them to a tailor to turn into a pair of shorts.

Sitaram, of course, was willing to lend me any number of trousers provided I wasn't fussy about who the owners were, and gave them back in time for them to be washed and pressed again before being delivered to their rightful owners. I did, on an occasion, borrow a pair made of a nice checked material, and was standing outside the Indiana, chatting to the owner, when I realized that he was staring hard at the trousers.

'I have a pair just like yours,' he remarked.

'It shows you have good taste,' I said, and gave Sitaram an earful when I got back to the flat.

'I can't trust you with other people's trousers!' I shouted. 'Couldn't you have lent me a pair belonging to someone who lives far from here?'

He was genuinely contrite. 'I was looking for the right size,' he said. 'Would you like to try a dhoti? You will look good in a dhoti. Or a lungi. There's a purple lungi here, it belongs to a sub-inspector of police.'

'A purple lungi? The police are human, after all.'

Yes, money talks—and it's usually saying goodbye.

A freelance writer can't tell what he's going to make from one month to the next. This uncertainty is part of the charm of the writing idyllic country cycle-ride had ended in disaster and tragedy.

Dehra's traffic is horrific today, but there was not much of it then, and at six in the morning the roads were deserted. In any case, I was soon out of the town and then I reached the tea-gardens. I stopped at a small wayside teashop for refreshment and while I was about to dip a hard bun in my tea, a familiar shadow fell across the table, and I looked up to see Sitaram grinning at me. I'd forgotten—he too had a cycle.

Dear friend and familiar! I did not know whether to be pleased or angry.

'My cycle is faster than yours,' he said.

'Well, then carry on riding it to Rishikesh. I'll try to keep up with you.'

He laughed. 'You can't escape me that way, writer-sahib. I'm hungry.'

'Have something, then.'

'We will practise for your birthday.' And he helped himself to a boiled egg, two buns and a sponge cake that looked as though it had been in the shop for a couple of years. If Sitaram can digest that, I thought, then he's a true survivor.

'Where are you going?' he asked, as I prepared to mount my cycle.

'Anywhere,' I said. 'As far as I feel like going.'

'Come, I will show you roads that you have never seen before.'

Were these prophetic words? Was I to discover new paths and new meanings courtesy the washerman's son?

'Lead on, light of my life,' I said, and he beamed and set off at a good speed so that I had trouble keeping up with him.

He left the main road, and took a bumpy, dusty path through a bamboo-grove. It was a fairly broad path and we could cycle side by side. It led out of the bamboo grove into an extensive tea-garden, then turned and twisted before petering out beside a small canal.

We rested our cycles against the trunk of a mango tree, and as we did so, a flock of green parrots, disturbed by our presence, flew out from the tree, circling the area and making a good deal of noise. In India, the land of the loudspeaker, even the birds have learnt to shout in order to be heard.

The parrots finally settled on another tree. The mangoes were beginning to form, but many would be bruised by the birds before they could fully ripen.

life, but it can also make for some nail-biting finishes when it comes to paying the rent, the food bill at Komal's, postage on my articles and correspondence, typing paper, toothpaste, socks, shaving soap, candles (there was no light in my room) and other necessities. And friends like William Matheson and Suresh Mathur (the only out-of-work lawyer I have ever known) did not make it any easier for me.

William, though Swiss, had served in the French Foreign Legion, and had been on the run in Vietnam along with the French administration and army once the Vietnamese had decided they'd had enough of the *Marseillaise*. The French are not known for their military prowess, although they would like to think otherwise.

William had drifted into Dehra as the assistant to a German newspaper correspondent, Von Radloff, who based his dispatches on the Indian papers and sent them out with a New Delhi dateline. Dehra was a little cooler than Delhi, and it was still pretty in parts. You could lead a pleasant life there, if you had an income.

William and Radloff fell out, and William decided he'd set up on his own as a correspondent. But there weren't many takers for his articles in

Europe, and his debts were mounting. He continued to live in an expensive guest house whose owner, an unusually tolerant landlord, reminded him one day that he was five months in arrears.

William took to turning up at my room around the same time as the postman, to see if I'd received any cheques or international money orders.

'Only pounds,' I told him one day. 'No French or Swiss francs. How could I possibly aspire to a French publisher?'

'Pounds will do. I owe my Sardarji about five thousand rupees.'

'Well, you'll have to keep owing him. My twelve pounds from the *Young Elizabethan* won't do much for you.'

The *Young Elizabethan* was a classy British children's magazine, edited by Kaye Webb and Pat Campbell. A number of my early stories found a home between its covers. Alas, like many other good things, it vanished a couple of years later. But in that golden year of my debut it was one of my mainstays.

'Why don't you look for cheaper accommodation?' I asked William.

'I have to keep up appearances. How can the correspondent of the Franco-German press live in a hovel like yours?'

'Well, suit yourself,' I said. 'I hope you get some money soon.'

All the same, I lent him two hundred rupees, and of course never saw it again. Would I have enough for my birthday party? That was now the burning question.

Five

Early one morning I decided I'd take a long cycle ride out of the town's precincts. I'd read all about the dawn coming up like thunder, but had never really got up early enough to witness it. I asked Sitaram to do me a favour and wake me at six. He woke me at five. It was just getting light. As I dressed, the colour of the sky changed from ultramarine to a clear shade of lavender, and then the sun came up gloriously naked.

I had borrowed a cycle from my landlady—it was occasionally used by her son or servant to deliver purchases to favoured customers—and I rode off down the Rajpur Road in a rather wobbly, zig-zag manner, as it was about five years since I had ridden a cycle. I was careful; I did not want to end up a cripple like Denton Welch, the sensitive author of A Voice in the Clouds, whose

idyllic country cycle-ride had ended in disaster and tragedy.

Dehra's traffic is horrific today, but there was not much of it then, and at six in the morning the roads were deserted. In any case, I was soon out of the town and then I reached the tea-gardens. I stopped at a small wayside teashop for refreshment and while I was about to dip a hard bun in my tea, a familiar shadow fell across the table, and I looked up to see Sitaram grinning at me. I'd forgotten—he too had a cycle.

Dear friend and familiar! I did not know whether to be pleased or angry.

'My cycle is faster than yours,' he said.

'Well, then carry on riding it to Rishikesh. I'll try to keep up with you.'

He laughed. 'You can't escape me that way, writer-sahib. I'm hungry.'

'Have something, then.'

'We will practise for your birthday.' And he helped himself to a boiled egg, two buns and a sponge cake that looked as though it had been in the shop for a couple of years. If Sitaram can digest that, I thought, then he's a true survivor.

'Where are you going?' he asked, as I prepared to mount my cycle.

'Anywhere,' I said. 'As far as I feel like going.'

'Come, I will show you roads that you have never seen before.'

Were these prophetic words? Was I to discover new paths and new meanings courtesy the washerman's son?

'Lead on, light of my life,' I said, and he beamed and set off at a good speed so that I had trouble keeping up with him.

He left the main road, and took a bumpy, dusty path through a bamboo-grove. It was a fairly broad path and we could cycle side by side. It led out of the bamboo grove into an extensive tea-garden, then turned and twisted before petering out beside a small canal.

We rested our cycles against the trunk of a mango tree, and as we did so, a flock of green parrots, disturbed by our presence, flew out from the tree, circling the area and making a good deal of noise. In India, the land of the loudspeaker, even the birds have learnt to shout in order to be heard.

The parrots finally settled on another tree. The mangoes were beginning to form, but many would be bruised by the birds before they could fully ripen.

A kingfisher dived low over the canal and came up with a little gleaming fish.

'Too tiny for us,' I said, 'or we might have caught a few.'

'We'll eat fish tikkas in the bazaar on our way back,' said Sitaram, a pragmatic person.

While Sitaram went exploring the canal banks, I sat down and rested my back against the bole of the mango tree.

A sensation of great peace stole over me. I felt in complete empathy with my surroundings— the gurgle of the canal water, the trees, the parrots, the bark of the tree, the warmth of the sun, the softness of the faint breeze, the caterpillar on the grass near my feet, the grass itself, each blade ... And I knew that if I always remained close to these things, growing things, the natural world, life would come alive for me, and I would be able to write as long as I lived.

Optimism surged through me, and I began singing an old song of Nelson Eddy's, a Vincent Huyman composition—

When you are down and out,
Lift up your head and shout—
It's going to be a great day!

Across the canal, moving through some wild babul trees, a dim figure seemed to be approaching. It wasn't the boy, it wasn't a stranger, it was someone I knew. Though he remained dim, I was soon able to recognize my father's face and form.

He stood there, smiling, and the song died on my lips.

But perhaps it was the song that had brought him back for a few seconds. He had always liked Nelson Eddy, collected his records. Where were they now? Where were the songs of old? The past has served us well; we must preserve all that was good in it.

As I stood up and raised my hand in greeting, the figure faded away.

My dear, dear father. How much I had loved him. And I had been only ten when he had been snatched away. Now he had given me a sign that he was still with me, would always be with me . . .

There was a great splashing close by, and I looked down to see that Sitaram was in the water. I hadn't even noticed him slip off his clothes and jump into the canal.

He beckoned to me to join him, and after a moment's hesitation, I decided to do so. Sitaram and I romped around in the waist-deep water for

quite some time. He was a beautiful glistening chocolate colour in the late morning sunshine. I would have to get into the open more often; I felt pale and washed out.

After some time I climbed the opposite bank and walked to the place where I had seen my father approaching. But there was no sign that anyone had been there. Not even a footprint.

SIX

It was mid-afternoon when we cycled back to the town. Siesta-time for many, but some brave souls were playing cricket on a vacant lot. There were spacious bungalows in the Dalanwala area; they had lawns and well-kept gardens. Dehra's establishment lived here. As did the Maharani of Magador, whose name-plate caught my eye as we rode slowly past the gate. I got off my cycle and stood at the kerb, looking over the garden wall.

'What are you looking at?' asked Sitaram, dismounting beside me.

'I want to invite the Maharani's daughter to my birthday party. But I don't suppose her mother will allow her to come.'

'Invite the mother too,' said Sitaram.

'Brilliant!' I said. 'Hit two Ranis with one stone.'

'Two birds in hand!' added Sitaram, who remembered his English proverbs from Class Seven. 'And look, there is one in the bushes!'

He pointed towards a hedge of hibiscus, where Indu was at work pruning the branches. Our voices had carried across the garden, and she looked up and stared at us for a few seconds before recognizing me. She walked slowly across the grass and stopped on the other side of the low wall, smiling faintly, looking from me to Sitaram and back to me.

'Hello,' she said. 'Where have you been cycling?'

'Oh, all over the place. Across the canal and into the fields like Hemingway. Now we're on our way home. Sitaram lives next door to me. When I saw your place, I thought I'd stop and say hello. Is your mother at home?'

'Yes, she's resting. Do you want to see her?'

'Er, no. Well, sure, but I won't disturb her. What I wanted to say was—if you're free on the 19th, come and join me and my friends for tea. It's my birthday, my twenty-first.'

'How nice. But my mother won't let me go alone.'

'The invitation includes her. If she comes, will you?'

'I'll ask her.'

I looked into her eyes. Deep brown, rather mischievous eyes. Were they responding to my look of gentle adoration? Or were they just amused because I was so self-conscious, so gauche? I could write stories, earn a living, converse with people from all walks of life, ride a bicycle, play football, climb trees, put back a few drinks, walk for miles without tiring, play with babies, charm grandmothers, impress fathers; but when it came to making an impression on the opposite sex, I was sadly out of depth, a complete dunce. It was I, not Indu, who had to hide the blushes ...

Even in London, two years earlier, when I had tried to prove my manhood by going to a prostitute in Leicester Square, everything had gone wrong. She had looked quite attractive under the street light where she had accosted me—or had I accosted her? But when she took me up to her room and exposed her flabby legs and thighs, I was repelled, mainly because she was suffering badly from varicose veins. You linger over your *Playboy* centre spreads, and then you go out and find your first woman, and she has varicose veins! I gave the unfortunate lady her fee and fled. But the smell of her powder and paint wouldn't leave my coat—my only coat—and I had to live with this failure for days!

The experience convinced me that I was more suited to romantic dalliance than sexual conquests, and that the latter would follow naturally from the former. My intentions towards Indu were perfectly honourable, although I couldn't see her mother accepting me into the royal fold. But perhaps one day when fame and fortune were mine (soon, I hoped!) Indu would give up her protected existence and come and live with me in a house by the sea or a villa on some tropical isle. I made up these lines on the spot, but held back from reciting them:

With the bougainvillaea in her hair
And blossoms on her breasts
My lips would search between her thighs for
    honeydew's caress . . .

As Indu gazed into my eyes, I said, quite boldly and to my own surprise, 'I have to kiss you one of these days, Indu.'

'Why not today?'

She was offering me her cheek, and that's where I started, but then she let me kiss her on her lips, and it was so sweet and intoxicating that when I felt someone pressing my hand I was sure it was Indu. I returned the pressure, then realized that Indu was on the other side of the wall, still holding the hedge-cutters. I'd quite forgotten Sitaram's presence. The pressure of his hand increased; I turned to look at him and he nodded approvingly. Indu had drawn away from the wall just as her mother's voice carried to us across the garden: 'Who are you talking to, Indu? Is it someone we know?'

'Just a college student!' Indu called back, and then, waving, walked slowly in the direction of the verandah. She turned once and said, 'I'll come to the party, mother too!'

And I was left with Sitaram holding my hand.

'Only one thing missing,' he said.

'What's that?'

'Filmi music.'

There was filmi music in full measure when we got to the Orient Cinema, where they were showing *Mr and Mrs 55* starring Madhubala, who was everybody's heart-throb that year. Sitaram insisted that I return my bicycle and join him in the cheap seats, which I did, almost passing out from the aromatic *beedi* smoke that filled the hall. The Orient had once shown English films, and I remembered seeing an early British comedy, *The Ghost of St. Michael's* (with Will Hay), when I was a boy. The front of the cinema, facing the parade-ground, was decorated with a bas-relief of dancers, designed by Sudhir Khastgir, art master at the Doon School, and they certainly lent character to the building—the rest of its character was fast disintegrating. But I enjoyed watching the crowd at the cinema. For me, the audience was always more interesting than the performers.

All I remember of the film was that Sitaram got very restless whenever Madhubala appeared on the screen. He would whistle along with the tongawallahs and squeeze my arm or other parts of my anatomy to indicate that he was really turned on by his favourite screen heroine. A good thing Madhubala wasn't coming to town, or there'd have been a riot; but for some time there had been a rumour that Prem Nath, a successful male star, would be visiting Dehra, and my landlady had been quite excited at the prospect. But Sitaram was not turned on by Prem Nath. It was Madhubala or nothing.

After the film, while wending our way through the bazaar, we were accosted by Jai Shankar, who walked with us to the Frontier Sweet Shop, where hot fresh jalebis were being dished out to the evening's first customers.

'Your turn to pay,' I said.

'Next time, next time,' promised the pride of the Doon School.

'I'm broke,' I said.

'Your friend must have some money.'

It turned out that Sitaram did possess a few crumpled notes, which he thrust into my hand.

'What does your friend do?' asked Jai.

'He's in the garment business,' I said.

Jai looked at Sitaram with renewed respect. When he'd had his fill of jalebis he insisted on showing us his new painting. So we walked home with him along his haunted alley, and he took us into his studio and proudly displayed a painting of a purple lady, very long in the arms and legs, and somewhat flat-chested.

'Well, what do you think?' asked Jai, standing back and looking at his bizarre creation with an affectionate eye.

'Are you doing it for your school founder's day?' I asked innocently.

'No, nudes aren't permitted. But you should see my study of angels in flight. It won the first prize!'

'Well, if you give this one a halo and wings, it could be an angel.'

Jai turned from me in disgust and asked Sitaram for his opinion.

Sitaram stared at the painting quizzically and said, 'She must have given all her clothes for washing.'

'There speaks the garment manufacturer,' I put in.

'The breasts could be bigger,' added Sitaram, as an afterthought.

'Maybe I will enlarge the breasts,' conceded Jai, with a thoughtful nod.

'Not too much,' I said. 'Large breasts are going out of fashion.'

'Why's that?'

'Too many males have them.'

Jai saw us to the door, but not down the dark alley; he never took it alone. All his life he was to be afraid of being alone in the dark. Well, we all have our phobias. To this day, I won't use a lift or escalator unless I have company.

Sitaram and I walked back quite comfortably

in the dark. He linked his fingers with mine and broke into song, a little off-key; he was no Saigal or Rafi. We cut across the *maidaan*, and a quarter-moon kept us company. I was overcome by a feeling of tranquility, a love for all the world, and wondered if it had something to do with the vision of my father earlier in the day.

As we climbed the steps to the landing that separated my rooms from Sitaram's quarters, we could hear his parents' voices raised in their nightly recriminations. His mother was a virago, no doubt; and his father was a drunk who gambled away most of his earnings. For Sitaram it was a trap from which there was only one escape. And he voiced my thought.

'I'll leave home one of these days,' he said.

'Well, tonight you can stay with me.'

I'd said it without any forethought, simply on an impulse. He followed me into my room, without bothering to inform his parents that he was back.

My landlady's large double-bed provided plenty of space for both of us. She hadn't used it since her husband's death, some six or seven years previously. And it was unlikely that she would be using it again.

Seven

Someone was getting married, and the wedding band, brought up on military marches, unwittingly broke into the *Funeral March*. And they played loud enough to wake the dead.

After a medley of Souza marches, they switched to Hindi film tunes, and Sitaram came in, flung his arms around and shattered my eardrums with Talat Mehmood's latest love ballad. I responded with the *Volga Boatmen* in my best Nelson Eddy manner, and my landlady came running out of her shop downstairs wanting to know if the washerman had strangled his wife or vice-versa.

Anyway, it was to be a week of celebrations . . .

When I opened my eyes next day, it was to find a bright red geranium staring me in the face, accompanied by the aromatic odour of a crushed geranium leaf. Sitaram was thrusting a potted geranium at me and wishing me a happy birthday. I brushed a caterpillar from my pillow and sat up. Wordsworthian though I was in principle, I wasn't prepared for nature red in tooth and claw.

I picked up the caterpillar on its leaf and dropped it outside.

'Come back when you're a butterfly,' I said.

Sitaram had taken his morning bath and looked very fresh and spry. Unfortunately, he had doused his head with some jasmine-scented hair oil, and the room was reeking of it. Already a bee was buzzing around him.

'Thank you for the present,' I said. 'I've always wanted a geranium.'

'I wanted to bring a rose-bush but the pot was too heavy.'

'Never mind. Geraniums do better on verandahs.'

I placed the pot in a sunny corner of the small balcony, and it certainly did something for the place. There's nothing like a red geranium for bringing a balcony to life.

While we were about to plan the day's festivities, a stranger walked through my open door (one day, I'd have to shut it), and declared himself the inventor of a new flush-toilet which, he said, would revolutionize the sanitary habits of the town. We were still living in the thunderbox era, and only the very rich could afford Western-style lavatories. My visitor showed me diagrams of a seat which, he said, combined the best of East and West. You could squat on it, Indian-style, without putting too much strain on your abdominal muscles, and if you used water to wash your bottom, there was a little sprinkler attached which, correctly aimed, would do that job for you. It was comfortable, efficient, safe. Your effluent would be stored in a little tank, which could be detached when full, and emptied—where? He hadn't got around to that problem as yet, but he assured me that his invention had a great future.

'But why are you telling me all this?' I asked, 'I can't afford a fancy toilet-seat.'

'No, no, I don't expect you to buy one.'

'You mean I should demonstrate?'

'Not at all. But you are a writer, I hear. I want a name for my new toilet-seat. Can you help?'

'Why not call it the Sit-Safe?' I suggested.

'The Sit-Safe! How wonderful. Young Mr Bond, let me show my gratitude with a small present.' And he thrust a ten-rupee note into my hand and left the room before I could protest. 'It's definitely my birthday,' I said. 'Complete strangers walk in and give me money.'

'We can see three films with that,' said Sitaram.

'Or buy three bottles of beer,' I said.

But there were no more windfalls that morning, and I had to go to the old Allahabad Bank—where my grandmother had kept her savings until they had dwindled away—and withdraw one hundred rupees.

'Can you tell me my balance?' I asked Mr Jain, the elderly clerk who remembered my maternal grandmother.

'Two hundred and fifty rupees,' he said with a smile. 'Try to save something!'

I emerged into the hot sunshine and stood on the steps of the bank, where I had stood as a small boy some fifteen years back, waiting for Granny to finish her work—I think she had been the only one in the family to put some money by for a rainy day—but these had been rainy days for her son and daughters and various fickle relatives who were always battening off her. Her own needs were few. She lived in one room of her house, leaving the rest of it for the family to use. When she died, the house was sold so that her children could once more go their impecunious ways.

I had no relatives to support, but here was William Matheson waiting for me under the old peepal tree. His hands were shaking.

'What's wrong?' I asked.

'Haven't had a cigarette for a week. Come on, buy me a packet of Charminar.'

Sitaram went out and bought samosas and jalebis and little cakes with icing made from solidified ghee. I fetched a few bottles of beer, some orangeades and lemonades and a syrupy cold drink called Vimto which was all the rage then. My landlady, hearing that I was throwing a party, sent me pakoras made with green chillies.

The party, when it happened, was something of an anticlimax:

Jai Shankar turned up promptly and ate all the jalebis.

William arrived with Suresh Mathur, finished the beer and demanded more.

Nobody paid much attention to Sitaram, he seemed so much at home. Caste didn't count for much in a fairly modern town, as Dehra was in those days. In any case, from the way Sitaram was strutting around, acting as though he owned the place, it was generally presumed that he was the landlady's son. He brought up a second relay of the lady's pakoras, hotter than the first lot, and they arrived just as the Maharani and Indu appeared in the doorway.

'Happy birthday, dear boy,' boomed the Maharani and seized the largest chilli pakora. Indu appeared behind her and gave me a box wrapped in gold and silver cellophane. I put it on my desk and hoped it contained chocolates, not studs and a tie-pin.

The chilli pakoras did not take long to violate the Maharani's taste-buds.

'Water, water!' she cried, and seeing the bathroom door open, made a dash for the tap.

Alas, the bathroom was the least attractive aspect of my flat. It had yet to be equipped with anything resembling the newly-invented Sit-Safe. But the lid of the thunderbox was fortunately down, as this particular safe hadn't been emptied for a couple of days. It was crowned by a rusty old tin mug. On the wall hung a towel that had seen better days. The remnants of a cake of Lifebuoy soap stood near a cracked washbasin. A lonely cockroach gave the Maharani a welcoming genuflection.

Taking all this in at a glance, she backed out, holding her hand to her mouth.

'Try a Vimto,' said William, holding out a bottle gone warm and sticky.

'A glass of beer?' asked Jai Shankar.

The Maharani grabbed a glass of beer and swallowed it in one long gulp. She came up gasping, gave me a reproachful look—as though the chilli pakora had been intended for her—and said, 'Must go now. Just stopped by to greet you. Thank you very much—you must come to Indu's birthday party. Next year.'

Next year seemed a long way off.

'Thank you for the present,' I said.

And then they were gone, and I was left to entertain my cronies.

Suresh Mathur was demanding something stronger than beer, and as I felt that way myself, we trooped off to the Royal Cafe; all of us, except Sitaram, who had better things to do.

After two rounds of drinks, I'd gone through

what remained of my money. And so I left William and Suresh to cadge drinks off one of the latter's clients, while I bid Jai Shankar goodbye on the edge of the parade-ground. As it was still light, I did not have to see him home.

Some workmen were out on the parade-ground, digging holes for tent-pegs.

Two children were discussing the coming attraction.

'The circus is coming!'

'Is it big?'

'It's the biggest! Tigers, elephants, horses, chimpanzees! Tight-rope walkers, acrobats, strong men . . .'

'Is there a clown?'

'There has to be a clown. How can you have a circus without a clown?'

I hurried home to tell Sitaram about the circus. It would make a change from the cinema. The room had been tidied up, and the Maharani's present stood on my desk, still in its wrapper.

'Let's see what's inside,' I said, tearing open the packet.

It was a small box of nuts—almonds, pistachios, cashew nuts, along with a few dried figs.

'Just a handful of nuts,' said Sitaram, sampling a fig and screwing up his face.

I tried an almond, found it was bitter and spat it out.

'Must have saved them from her wedding day,' said Sitaram.

'Appropriate in a way,' I said. 'Nuts for a bunch of nuts.'

Eight

Lines written on a hot summer's night:

> On hot summer nights I dream
> Of you beside me, near a mountain stream
> Cool in our bed of ferns we lie,
> Lost in our loving, as the world slips by.

I tried to picture Indu in my arms, the two of us watching the moon come over the mountains. But her face kept dissolving and turning into her mother's. This transition from dream to nightmare kept me from sleeping. Sitaram slept peacefully at the edge of the bed, immune to the mosquitoes that came in like squadrons of dive-bombers. It was much too hot for any body contact, but even then, the sheets were soaked with perspiration.

Tired of his parents' quarrels, and his father's constant threat of turning him out if he did not start contributing towards the family's earnings, Sitaram was practically living with me. I had been on my own for the past five years and had grown used to a form of solitary confinement. I don't think I could have shared my life with an intellectual companion. William and Jai Shankar were stimulating company in the Indiana or Royal Cafe, but I doubt if I would have enjoyed waking up to their argumentative presences first thing every morning. William disagreed with everything I wrote or said; I was too sentimental, too whimsical, too descriptive. He was probably right, but I preferred to write in the manner that gave me the maximum amount of enjoyment. There was more give and take with Jai, but I knew he'd be writing a thousand words to my hundred, and this would have been a little disconcerting to a lazy writer.

Sitaram made no demands on my intellect. He left me to my writing-pad and typewriter. As a physical presence, he was acceptable and grew more interesting by the day. He ran small errands for me, accompanied me on the bicycle-rides which often took us past the Maharani's house. And he took an interest in converting the small balcony into a garden—so much so, that my landlady began complaining that water was seeping through the floor and dripping on to the flour sacks in her ration shop.

The red geranium was joined by a cerise one, and I wondered where it had come from, until I heard the Indiana proprietor complaining that one of his pots was missing.

A potted rose-plant, neglected by Suresh Mathur (who neglected his clients with much the same single-minded carelessness) was appropriated and saved from a slow and lingering death. Subjected to cigarette butts, the remnants of drinks and half-eaten meals, it looked as though it would never produce a rose. So it made the journey from Suresh's verandah to mine without protest from its owner (since he was oblivious of its presence) and under Sitaram's ministrations soon perked up and put forth new leaves and a bud.

My landlady had thrown out a wounded succulent, and this too found a home on the balcony, along with a sickly asparagus-fern left with me by William.

A plant hospital, no less!

Coming up the steps one evening, I was struck by the sweet smell of *raat-ki-rani*, Queen of the Night, and I was puzzled by its presence because I knew there was none growing on our balcony or anywhere else in the vicinity. In front of the building stood a neem tree, and a mango tree, the last survivor of the mango grove that had occupied this area before it was cleared away for a shopping block. There were no shrubs around—they would not have survived the traffic or the press of people. Only potted plants occupied the shopfronts and verandah-spaces. And yet there was that distinct smell of raat-ki-rani, growing stronger all the time.

Halfway up the steps, I looked up, and saw my father standing at the top of the steps, in the half-light of a neighbouring window. He was looking at me the way he had done that day near the canal—with affection and a smile playing on his lips—and at first I stood still, surprised by happiness. Then, waves of love and the old companionship sweeping over me, I advanced up the steps; but when I reached the top, the vision faded and I stood there alone, the sweet smell of raat-ki-rani still with me, but no one else, no sound but the distant shunting of an engine.

This was the second time I'd seen my father, or rather his apparition, and I did not know if it portended anything, or if it was just that he wanted to see me again, was trying to cross the gulf between our different worlds, the worlds of yesterday, today and tomorrow.

Alone on the balcony, looking down at the badly-lit street, I indulged in a bout of nostalgia, recalling boyhood days when my father was my only companion—in the RAF tent outside Delhi, with the hot winds of May and June swirling outside; then the cool evening walks in Chotta Shimla, on the road to Bishop Cotton School; and earlier, exploring the beach at Jamnagar, picking up and storing away different kinds of seashells.

I still had one with me—a smooth round shell which must have belonged to a periwinkle. I put it to my ear and heard the hum of the ocean, the siren song of the sea. I knew that one day I would have to choose between the sea and the mountains, but for the moment it was this little sub-tropical valley, hot and humid, patiently waiting for the monsoon rains . . .

The mango trees were sweet with blossom. 'My love is like a red, red rose,' sang Robbie Burns, while John Clare, another poet of the countryside, declared: 'My love is like a bean-field in blossom.' In India, sweethearts used to meet in the mango-groves at blossom time. They don't do that any more. Mango-groves are no longer private places. Better a dark corner of the Indiana, with Larry Gomes playing old melodies on his piano . . .

I walked down to A.N. John's saloon for a haircut, but couldn't get anywhere near the entrance. An excited but good-natured crowd had taken up most of the narrow road as well as a resident's front garden.

'What's happening?' I asked a man who was selling candyfloss.

'Dilip Kumar is inside. He's having a haircut.'

Dilip Kumar! The most popular male star of the silver screen!

'But what's he doing in Dehra?' I asked.

The candyfloss-seller looked at me as though I was a cretin. 'I just told you—having a haircut.'

I moved on to where the owner of the bicycle-hire shop was standing. 'What's Dilip Kumar doing in town?' I asked. He shrugged. 'Don't know. Must be something to do with the circus.'

'Is he the ringmaster for the circus?' asked a little boy in a pyjama suit.

'Of course not,' said the pigtailed girl beside him. 'The circus won't be able to pay him enough.'

'Maybe he owns the circus,' said the little boy.

'It belongs to a friend of his,' said a tongawallah with a knowing air. 'He's come for the opening night.'

Whatever the reasons for Dilip Kumar's presence in Dehra, it was agreed by all that he was in A.N. John's, having a haircut. There was only one way out of A.N. John's and that was by the front door. There were a couple of windows on either side, but the crowd had them well covered.

Finally the star emerged; beaming, waving to people, looking very handsome indeed in a white bush shirt and neatly pressed silvery grey trousers. There was a nice open look about him. No histrionics. No impatience to get away. He was the ordinary guy who'd made good.

Where was Sitaram? Why wasn't my star-struck friend in the crowd? I found him later, watching the circus tents go up, but by then Dilip Kumar was on his way to Delhi. He hadn't come for the circus at all. He'd been visiting his young friend Nandu Jauhar at the Savoy in neighbouring Mussoorie.

Nine

The circus opened on time, and the parade-ground became a fairy land of lights and music. This happened only once in every five years when the Great Gemini Circus came to town. This particular circus toured every town, large and small, throughout the length and breadth of India, so naturally it took some time for it to return to scenes of past triumphs; and by the time it did so, some of the acts had changed, younger performers had taken the place of some of the older ones, and a new generation of horses, tigers and elephants were on display. So, in effect, it was a brand new circus in Dehra, with only a few familiar faces in the ring or on the trapeze.

The senior clown was an old-timer who'd been to Dehra before, and he welcomed the audience with a flattering little speech which was cut short when one of the prancing ponies farted full in his face. Was this accident or design? We in the audience couldn't tell, but we laughed all the same.

A circus does bring all kinds of people together under the one tent-top. The popular stands were of course packed, but the more expensive seats were also occupied. I caught sight of Indu and her mother. They were accompanied by someone who looked like the Prince of Purkazi. I looked again, and came to the conclusion that it was indeed the Prince of Purkazi. A pang of jealously assailed me. What was the eligible young prince doing in the company of my princess? Why wasn't he playing cricket for India or the minor counties, or preferably on some distant field in east UP where bottles and orange-peels would be showered down on the players? Could the Maharani be scheming to get him married to her daughter? The dreadful thought crossed my mind.

He was handsome, he was becoming famous, he was royalty. And he probably owned race-horses.

But not the ones in the circus-ring. They looked reasonably well-fed, and they were obedient; but they weren't of racing stock. A gentle canter around the ring had them snorting and heaving at the flanks as though they'd just finished running all the way from Meerut, their last stop.

Dear Nergis Dalal was watching them with her eagle eye. She was just starting out on her campaign for the SPCA, with particular reference to circus animals, and she had her notebook and fountain-pen poised and ready for action. Nergis, then in her thirties, had come into prominence after winning a newspaper short story contest, and her articles and middles were now appearing quite regularly in the national press. She knew William Matheson and disapproved of him, for he was known to move around in a pony trap. She knew Suresh Mathur and disapproved of him; he had shot his neighbour's Dobermann for howling beneath his window all night. She disapproved of the Indiana owner for serving up partridges at Christmas. And did she disapprove of me? Not yet. But I could sense her looking my way to see if I was enjoying the show. That would have gone against me. So I pretended to look bored; then turned towards her with a resigned look and threw my arms up in the air in a sort of world-weary gesture. 'I'm here for the same reasons as you,' was what it meant, and I must have succeeded, because she gave me a friendly nod. Quite a decent sort, Nergis.

There were several other acquaintances strewn about the audience, including a pale straw-haired boy called Tom Alter, who had managed to secure Dilip Kumar's autograph earlier that day. Tom was the son of American missionaries, but his heart was in Hindi movies and already he was nursing an ambition to be a film star.

William and Jai were absent. They felt the circus was just a little below their intellectual brows. Jai said he had a painting to finish, and William was writing a long article on one of the country's Five-Year Plans—don't ask me which one ... At the time a writer named Khushwant Singh was editing a magazine called *Yojana*, which was all about Five-Year Plans, and he had asked William to do the article. I'd offered the editor an article on punch and its five ingredients—spirit, lemon or lime juice, spice, sugar and rose water—but had been politely turned down. Mr Singh liked his Scotch, but punch was not within the purview of the Five-Year Plan.

To return to the circus ... The trapeze artistes (from Kerala) were very good. The girl on the tight rope (from Andhra) was scintillating in her skin-tight, blue-sequinned costume. The lady lion-tamer (from Tamil Nadu) was daunting, although her lion did look a bit scruffy. The talent seemed to come largely from the south, so that it did not surprise me when the band broke into that lovely Strauss waltz, *Roses of the South*.

The ringmaster came from Bengal. He had a snappy whip, and its sound, as it whistled through the air, was sufficient to command obedience from snarling tigers, prancing ponies and dancing bears. He did not actually touch anyone with it. The whistle of the whip was sufficient.

Sitaram, who sat beside me looking like Sabu in *The Thief of Baghdad*, was enthralled by all he saw. This was his first circus, and every single act and individual performance had his complete attention. His face was suffused with delighted anticipation. He gasped when the trapeze artistes flew through the air. He laughed at the clown's antics. He sang to the tunes the band played, and he whistled (along with the rowdier sections of the audience) when those alluring southern beauties stood upright on their cantering, wheeling ponies—oh, to be a pony!

Oh, to be a pony
With a girl upon my rump,

And I'll take you round the ring, my dear,
Without a single bump.

Not one of my best efforts, but it came to me
on the spur of the moment and I said it out loud
for the benefit of Sitaram.

'Nice song,' he said. 'I like the one on the
second pony. Isn't she beautiful?'

'Stunning,' I agreed. 'I like the sparkle in her
eyes.'

'Sparkling eyes are for the poets,' said Sitaram,
always bringing me back to earth. 'I like her
thighs. Say something about her thighs, poet.'

'Her thighs are like melons—' I began.

'Not melons! I hate melons. They grow all
over the *dhobi-ghat*.'

'Sorry, friend. Like half-moons? You like
moons?'

'Yes. And her lips?'

'Like rosebuds.'

'Rosebuds. Good. And her breasts?'

'Well, in the frilled costume she's wearing,
they look like cabbages.'

Sitaram pinched my thigh, fiercely, so that it
hurt. But he wasn't angry. His gaze followed the
girl on the pony until she, along with the others
in the act, made their exit from the ring.

There were a number of other interesting acts—a dare-devil motor-cyclist riding through a ring of fire, the lady-wrestler taking on a rather somnolent bear and three tigers forming a sort of pyramid atop a revolving platform—but Sitaram was only half-attentive, his thoughts still being with the beautiful, dark, pink-sequinned girl on her white pony.

On the way home he held my hand and sighed.

'I have to go again tomorrow,' he said. 'You'll lend me the money won't you? I have to see that girl again.'

Ten

For a couple of weeks Sitaram was busy with the circus, and I did not see much of him. When he wasn't watching the evening performance, he was there in the mornings, hanging round the circus tents, trying to strike up an acquaintance with the ring-hands or minor performers. Most of the artistes and performers were staying in cheap hotels near the railway station. Sitaram appointed himself an unofficial messenger boy, and as he was familiar with every corner of the town, the circus people found him quite useful. He told them where they could get their clothes stitched or repaired, dry-cleaned or laundered; he guided them to the best eating-places, cheap but substantial restaurants such as Komal's or Chacha-da-Hotel (no Indiana or Royal Cafe for the circus crew); posted their letters home; found them barbers and masseurs; brought them newspapers. He was even able to get a copy of the *Madras Mail* for the lady lion-tamer.

Late one night (it must have been after the night show was over) he woke me from a deep dreamless sleep and without any preamble stuffed a laddoo into my mouth. Laddoos are not my favourite sweetmeat, and certainly not in bed at midnight, when the crumbs on the bedsheet were likely to attract an army of ants. While I was still choking on the laddoo, he gave me his good news.

'I've got a job at the circus!'

'What, as assistant to the clown?'

'No, not yet. But the manager likes me. He's made me his office boy. Two hundred rupees a month!'

'Almost as much as I make—but I suppose you'll be running around at all hours. And have you met the girl you liked—the dark girl on the white pony?'

'I have spoken to her. She smiles whenever she sees me. I have spoken to all the girls. They are very nice—especially the ones from the south.'

'Well, you're luckier than I am with girls.'

'Would you like to meet the lady wrestler?'

'The one who wrestles with the bear every night? After that, would she have any time for mere men?'

'They say she's in love with the ringmaster, Mr Victor. He uses his whip if she gets too rough.'

'I don't want to have anything to do with lady wrestlers, lions, bears or whips. Now let me go to sleep. I have to write a story in the morning. Something romantic.'

'What are you calling it?'

'"The Night Train at Deoli." Now go to sleep.'

He leant over and gave me a quick sharp bite on the cheek. I yelped.

'What's that supposed to be?' I demanded.

'That's how tigers make love,' he said, and vanished into the night.

The monsoon was only a fortnight away, we were told, and we were all looking forward to some relief from the hot and dusty days of June. Sometimes the nights were even more unbearable, as squadrons of mosquitoes came zooming across the eastern Doon. In those days the eastern Doon was more malarious than the western, probably because it was low-lying in parts and there was more still water in drains and pools. Wild boar and swamp deer abounded.

But it was now mango-time, and this was one of the compensations of summer. I kept a bucket filled with mangoes and dipped into it frequently during the day. So did Jai Shankar, William, Suresh Mathur and others who came by.

One of my more interesting visitors was a writer called G.V. Desani who had, a few years earlier, written a comic novel called *All About H. Hatterr*. I suspect that the character of Hatterr was based on Desani himself, for he was an eccentric individual who told me that he slept in a coffin.

'Do you carry it around with you?' I asked, over a coffee at Indiana.

'No, hotels won't allow me to bring it into the lobby, let alone my room. Hotel managers have a morbid fear of death, haven't they?'

'A coffin should make a good coffee-table. We'll put it to the owner of the Indiana.'

'Trains are fussy too. You can't have it in your compartment, and in the brake-van it gets smashed. Mine's an expensive mahogany coffin, lined with velvet.'

'I wish you many comfortable years sleeping in it. Do you intend being buried in it too?'

'No, I shall be cremated like any other good Hindu. But I may *will* the coffin to a good Christian friend. Would you like it?'

'I rather fancy being cremated myself. I'm not a very successful Christian. A pagan all my life. Maybe I'll get religious when I'm older.'

Mr Desani then told me that he was nominating his own novel for the Nobel Prize, and would I sign a petition that was to be presented to the Nobel Prize Committee extolling the merits of his book? Gladly, I said; always ready to help a good cause. And did I know of any other authors or patrons of literature who might sign? I told him there was Nergis Dalal; and William Matheson, an eminent Swiss Journalist; and old Mrs D' Souza who did a gardening column for *Eve's Weekly*; and Holdsworth, at the Doon School—he'd climbed Kamet with Frank Smythe, and had written an account for the journal of the Bombay Natural History Society— and of course there was Jai Shankar who was keeping a diary in the manner of Stendhal; and wasn't Suresh Mathur planning to write a Ph.D on P.G. Wodehouse? I gave their names and addresses to the celebrated author, and even added that of the inventor of the Sit-Safe. After all, hadn't he encouraged this young writer by commissioning him to write a brochure for his toilet-seat?

Mr Desani produced his own brochure, with quotes from reviewers and writers who had praised his work. I signed his petition and allowed him to pay for the coffee.

As I walked through the swing doors of the Indiana, Indu and her mother walked in. It was too late for me to turn back. I bowed like the gentleman my grandmother had always wanted me to be, and held the door for them, while they breezed in to the restaurant. Larry Gomes was playing *Smoke Gets in Your Eyes* with a wistful expression.

Eleven

Lady Wart of Worcester, Lady Tryiton and the Earl of Stopwater, the Hon. Robin Crazier, Mr and Mrs Paddy Snott-Noble, the Earl and Countess of Lost Marbles and General Sir Peter de l'Orange-Peel . . .

These were only some of the gracious names that graced the pages of the Doon Club's guest and membership register at the turn of the century, when the town was the favourite retiring place for the English aristocracy. So well did the Club look after its members that most of them remained permanently in Dehra, to be buried in the Chandernagar cemetery just off the Hardwar Road.

My own ancestors were not aristocracy. Dad's father came to India as an eighteen-year-old soldier in a Scots Regiment, a contemporary of Kipling's 'Soldiers Three'—Privates Othenis,

Mulvaney and Learoyd. He married an orphaned girl who had been brought up on an indigo plantation at Motihari in Bihar. My maternal grandfather worked in the Indian Railways, as a foreman in the railway workshops at some god-forsaken railway junction in central India. He married a statuesque, strong-willed lady who had also grown up in India. Dad was born in the Shahjahanpur military camp; my mother in Karachi. So although my forebears were, for the most part, European, I was third generation India-born. The expression, 'Anglo-Indian', has come to mean so many things—British settler, Old Koi-Hai, Colonel Curry or Captain Chapatti, or simply Eurasian—that I don't use it very often. Indian is good enough for me. I may have relatives scattered around the world, but I have no great interest in meeting them. My feet are firmly planted in Ganges soil.

Grandfather (of the Railways) retired in Dehradun (or Deyrah Dhoon, as it was spelt in the old days) and built a sturdy bungalow on the Old Survey Road. Sadly, it was sold at the time of Independence when most of his children decided to quit the country. After my father's death, my mother married a Punjabi gentleman and so I stayed on in India, except for that brief sojourn in England and the Channel Islands. I'd come back to Dehra to find that even mother and stepfather had left, but it was still home, and in the cemetery there were several relatives including Grandfather and Great-grandmother. If I sat on their graves, I felt I owned a bit of property. Not a bungalow or even a vegetable patch, but a few feet of well-nourished sod. There were even marigolds flowering at the edges of the graves. And a little blue everlasting that I have always associated with Dehra. It grows in ditches, on vacant plots, in neglected gardens, along footpaths, on the edges of fields, behind lime-kilns, wherever there is a bit of wasteland. Call it a weed if you like, but I have every respect for a plant that will survive the onslaught of brick, cement, petrol fumes, grazing cows and goats, heat and cold (for it flowers almost all the year round) and overflowing sewage. As long as that little flowering weed is still around, there is hope for both man and nature.

A feeling of tranquility and peace always pervaded my being when I entered the cemetery. Were my long-gone relatives pleased by my presence there? I did not see them in any form, but then, cemeteries are the last place for departed souls to hang around in. Given a chance, they would rather be among the living, near those they cared for or in places where they were happy. I have never been convinced by ghost stories in which the tormented spirit revisits the scene of some ghastly tragedy. Why on earth (or why in heaven) should they want to relive an unpleasant experience?

My maternal grandfather, by my mother's account, was a man with a sly sense of humour who often discomfited his relatives by introducing into their homes odd creatures who refused to go away. Hence the tiny Jharipani bat released into Aunt Mabel's bedroom, or the hedgehog slipped between his brother Major Clerke's bedsheets. A cousin, Mrs Blanchette, found her house swarming with white rats, while a neighbour received a gift of a parcel of papayas—and in their midst, a bright green and yellow chameleon.

And so, when I was within some fifty to sixty feet of Grandfather's grave, I was not in the least surprised to see a full-grown tiger stretched out on his tombstones apparently enjoying the shade of the magnolia tree which grew beside it.

Was this a manifestation of the tiger cub he'd kept when I was a child? Did the ghosts of long-dead tigers enjoy visiting old haunts? Live tigers certainly did, and when this one stirred, yawned and twitched its tail, I decided I wouldn't stay to find out if it was a phantom tiger or a real one.

Beating a hasty retreat to the watchman's quarters near the lych-gate, I noticed that a large, well-fed and very real goat was tethered to one of the old tombstones (Colonel Ponsonby of Her Majesty's Dragoons), and I concluded that the tiger had already spotted it and was simply building up an appetite before lunch.

'There's a tiger on Grandfather's grave,' I called out to the watchman, who was checking out his cabbage patch. (And healthy cabbages they were, too.)

The watchman was a bit deaf and assumed that I was complaining about some member of his family, as they were in the habit of grinding their masalas on the smoother gravestones.

'It's that boy Masood,' he said. 'I'll get after him with a stick.' And picking up his lathi, he made for the grave.

A yell, a roar, and the watchman was back and out of the lych-gate before me.

'Send for the police, sahib,' he shouted. 'It's one of the circus tigers. It must have escaped!'

Twelve

Sincerely hoping that Sitaram had not been in the way of the escaping tiger, I made for the circus tents on the parade-ground. There was no show in progress. It was about noon, and everyone appeared to be resting. If a tiger was missing, no one seemed to be aware of it.

'Where's Sitaram?' I asked one of the hands.

'Helping to wash down the ponies,' he replied.

But he wasn't in the pony enclosure. So I made my way to the rear, where there was a cage housing a lion (looking rather sleepy, after its late-night bout with the lady lion-tamer), another cage housing a tiger (looking ready to bite my head off) and another cage with its door open—empty!

Someone came up behind me, whistling cheerfully. It was Sitaram.

'Do you like the tigers?' he asked.

'There's only one here. There are three in the show, aren't there?'

'Of course, I helped feed them this morning.'

'Well, one of them's gone for a walk. Someone must have unlocked the door. If it's the same tiger I saw in the cemetery, I think it's looking for another meal—or maybe just dessert!'

Sitaram ran back into the tent, yelling for the trainer and the ringmaster. And then, of course, there was commotion. For no one had noticed the tiger slipping away. It must have made off through the bamboo-grove at the edge of the parade-ground, through the Forest Rangers College (well-wooded then), circled the police lines and entered the cemetery. By now it could have been anywhere.

It was, in fact, walking right down the middle of Dehra's main road, causing the first hold-up in traffic since Pandit Nehru's last visit to the town. Mr Nehru would have fancied the notion; he was keen on tigers. But the citizens of Dehra took no chances. They scattered at the noble beast's approach. The Delhi bus came to a grinding halt, while tonga-ponies, never known to move faster than a brisk trot, broke into a gallop that would have done them proud at the Bangalore Races.

The only creature that failed to move was a large bull (the one that someimes blocked the approach to my steps) sitting in the middle of the road, forming a traffic island of its own. It did not move for cars, buses, tongas and trucks. Why budge for a mere tiger?

And the tiger, having been fed on butcher's meat for most of its life, now disdained the living thing (since the bull refused to be stalked) and headed instead for the back entrance to the Indiana's kitchens.

There was a general exodus from the Indiana. William Matheson, who had been regaling his friends with tales of his exploits in the Foreign Legion, did not hang around either; he made for the comparative safety of my flat. Larry Gomes stopped in the middle of playing the *Anniversary Waltz*, and fox-trotted out of the restaurant. The owner of the Indiana rushed into the street and collided with the owner of the Royal Cafe. Both swore at each other in choice Pashtu—they were originally from Peshawar. Swami Aiyar, a Doon School boy with ambitions of being a newspaper correspondent, buttonholed me near my landlady's shop and asked me if I knew Jim Corbett's telephone number in Haldwani.

'But he only shoots man-eaters,' I protested.

'Well, they're saying three people have already been eaten in the bazaar.'

'Ridiculous. No self-respecting tiger would go for a three-course meal.'

'All the same, people are in danger.'

'So, we'll send for Jim Corbett. Aurora of the Green Bookshop should have his number.'

Mr Aurora was better informed than either of us. He told us that Jim Corbett had settled in Kenya several years ago.

Swami looked dismayed. 'I thought he loved India so much that he refused to leave.'

'You're confusing him with Jack Gibson of the Mayo School,' I said.

At this point the tiger came through the swing doors of the Indiana and started crossing the road. Suresh Mathur was driving slowly down Rajpur Road in his 1936 Hillman. He'd been up half the night, drinking and playing cards, and he had a terrible hangover. He was now heading for the Royal Cafe, convinced that only a chilled beer could help him recover. When he saw the tiger, his reflexes—never very good—failed him completely, and he drove his car onto the pavement and into the plate-glass window of Bhai Dhian Singh's Wine and Liquor Shop. Suresh looked quite happy among the broken rum bottles. The heady aroma of XXX Rosa Rum, awash on the shopping verandah, was too much for a couple of old topers, who began to mop up the liquor with their handkerchiefs. Suresh would have done the same had he been conscious.

We carried him into the deserted Indiana and sent for Dr Sharma.

'Nothing much wrong with him,' said the doctor, 'but he looks anaemic,' and proceeded to give him an injection of vitamin B12. This was Dr Sharma's favourite remedy for anyone who was ailing. He was a great believer in vitamins.

I don't know if the B12 did Suresh any good, but the jab of the needle woke him up, and he looked around, blinked up at me and said, 'Thought I saw a tiger. Could do with a drink, old boy.'

'I'll stand you a beer,' I said. 'But you'll have to pay the bill at Bhai Dhian's. And your car needs repairs.'

'And this injection costs five rupees,' said Dr Sharma.

'Beer is the same price. I'll stand you one too.'

So we settled down in the Indiana and finished several bottles of beer, Dr Sharma expounding all the time on the miracle of Vitamin B12, while Suresh told me that he knew now what it felt like to enter the fourth dimension.

The tiger was soon forgotten, and when I walked back to my room a couple of hours later and found the postman waiting for me with a twenty-five rupee money-order from *Sainik Samachar* (the Armed Forces' weekly magazine), I tipped him five rupees and put the rest aside for a rainy day—which, hopefully, would be the morrow, as monsoon clouds had been advancing from the south.

They say that those with a clear conscience usually sleep well. I have always done a lot of sleeping, especially in the afternoons, and have never been unduly disturbed by pangs of conscience, for I haven't deprived any man of his money, his wife or his song.

I kicked off my chappals and lay down and allowed my mind to dwell on my favourite Mexican proverb: 'How sweet it is to do nothing, and afterwards to rest!'

I hoped the tiger had found a shady spot for his afternoon siesta. With goodwill towards one and all, I drifted into a deep sleep and woke only in the early evening, to the sound of distant thunder.

Thirteen

The tiger padded silently but purposefully past the Dilaram Bazaar, paying no attention to the screaming and shouting of the little gesticulating creatures who fled at his approach. He'd seen them every night at the circus—all in search of excitement, provided there was no risk attached to it!

Walking down from the other end of the Dilaram Road was a tiger of another sort—sub-lnspector Sher ('Tiger') Singh, in charge of the local police outpost. 'Tiger Singh' was feeling on the top of the world. His little thana was notorious for beating up suspected criminals, and he'd had a satisfying night supervising the third-degree interrogation of three young suspects in a case of theft. None of them had broken down and confessed, but 'Tiger' had the pleasure (and what was it if not a pleasure, an appeal to his senses?) of kicking one youth senseless, blackening the eyes of another and fracturing the ankle and shinbone of the third. The damage done, they had been ejected into the street with a warning to keep their noses clean in the future.

These young men could have saved themselves from physical injury had they disbursed a couple of hundred rupees to the sub-inspector and his cohorts, but they were unemployed and without friends of substance; so, beaten and humiliated, they crawled home as best they could. 'Tiger' Singh liked the money he sometimes picked up from suspects and the relatives of petty offenders; but many years in the service had brought out the sadistic side to his nature, and now he took a certain pleasure in seeing noses broken and teeth knocked out. He claimed that he could extract teeth without anaesthesia, and would do the job free for those who could not afford dentists' bills. There were no takers.

Today he strutted along the pavement, twirling his moustaches with one hand and pulling up his trousers with the other. For he was a well-fed gentleman, whose belly protruded above his belt. He had a constant struggle keeping his trousers, along with his heavy revolver holster, from slipping to the ground. Had he not been in the direct path of the tiger, he would have been ignored. But he chose to stand frozen to the ground, really too terrified to reach for his gun or even hitch up his trousers.

The tiger slapped him to the ground, picked him up by his fat neck and dragged him into the lantana bushes. Sher Singh let out one despairing cry, which turned into a gurgle as the blood spurted from his throat.

The tiger did not eat humans. Their flesh was unappetizing, acceptable only to the lame or ageing beasts who could no longer hunt. True, the circus tiger had almost forgotten how to hunt, but his instincts told him that more succulent repasts could be found in the depths of the forest. And the forest was close at hand (or so it was in those days), so he abandoned the dead policeman, who would have made a more suitable meal for vultures had not his colleagues come and taken him away.

The autopsy report said, 'Killed by wild tiger,' which was inaccurate in that the tiger was tame, but it was the only extenuating remark ever made about the sub-inspector. His family received a pension and lived fairly happily ever after.

Neither the tiger nor the S.I. was familiar with the Laws of Karma, or Emerson's Law of Compensation, but they appeared to have been working all the same.

⌒

As the tiger sought its freedom in the forest, the clouds that had gathered over the foothills finally gave way under their burden of moisture. The first rain of the monsoon descended upon the hills, the valley, the town. In minutes, a two-month layer of dust was washed away from trees, rooftops and pavements. The rain swept across the streets of Dehra, sending people scattering for shelter. Umbrellas unfolded for the first time in months. A gust of wind shook the circus tent. The old lion, scenting the rain on the wind, sat up in its cage and gave a great roar of delight. The ponies shook their manes, an elephant trumpeted. One of the dwarves, who had been making love to the lady-wrestler, now did so with greater abandon. The ravished lady squealed with pleasure; for it has to be said that the dwarf was undersized in every department but one, and in that one area few could surpass him.

The rain swept over the railway yards, washing the soot and dust from the carriages and engines. It brought freshness and new life to the tea-gardens and sugarcane fields. Even earthworms responded to the cool dampening of their environment and stretched sensuously in the soft mud.

Mud! Buffaloes wallowed in it; children romped in it; frogs broke into antiphonal chants. Glorious, squelchy mud. Hateful for the rest of the year, but wonderfully inviting on the first day of the monsoon. A large amount got washed down from the loose eroded soil of the foothills, so that the streams and canals were soon clogged, silted up and flooded their banks.

The mango and litchi trees were washed clean. Sal and shisham shook in the wind. Peepal leaves danced. The roots of the banyan drank up the good rain. The neem gave out its heady fragrance. Squirrels ran for shelter into the embracing branches of Krishna's buttercup. Parrots made merry in the guava groves.

I walked home through the rain. Home, did I say? Yes, my small flat was becoming a home, what with Sitaram and his geraniums upstairs, my landlady below and other familiars in the neighbourhood. Even the geckos on the wall were now recognizable, each acquiring an identity and personality of its own. Sitaram had trained one of them to take food from his fingers. At first he had stuck a bit of meat at the end of a long thin stick. The lizard had snapped up this morsel. Then, every day, he had shortened the stick until the lizard, growing in confidence, took his snack from the short end of the stick and finally from the boy's fingers. I hadn't got around to feeding the wall lizards. One of them had fallen with a plop on my forehead in the middle of the night, and my landlady told me of how a whole family had been poisoned when a gecko had fallen into a cooking pot and been served up with a mixed vegetable curry.

A neighbour, who worked for Madras Coffee House, told me that down south there were a number of omens connected with the fall of the wall lizard, especially if it dropped on some part of your body. He told me that I'd been fortunate that the lizard fell on my forehead, but had it fallen on my tummy I'd have been in for a period of bad luck. But I wasn't taking any chances. The lizards could have all the snacks they wanted from Sitaram, but I wasn't going to encourage any familiarity.

Now, happy to get my clothes wet with the first monsoon shower, I ran up the steps to my rooms, but found them empty. Then Sitaram's voice, raised in song, wafted down to me from the rooftop. I climbed up to the roof by means of an old iron ladder that was always fixed there, and found him on the flat roof, prancing about in the nude.

'Come and join me,' he shouted. 'It is good to dance in the first monsoon shower.'

'You can be seen from the roofs across the road,' I said.

'Never mind. Don't you think I'm the sexiest man of 1955?'

'I shall look forward to seeing you in 1956,' I said, and retreated below.

Fourteen

It was still 1955, and the middle of the monsoon, when Sitaram decided to throw his lot in with the circus and leave Dehra. Those roses of the south had a lot to do with it. I wasn't sure if he was in love with one of the pony-riders, or with the girl on the flying trapeze.

Perhaps both of them; perhaps all of them. He was at an age when his sexual energies had to be directed somewhere, and those beautiful dusky circus girls were certainly more approachable, and more glamorous, than the coy college girls we saw every day.

'So you're going to desert me,' I said, when he told me of his plans.

'Only for a few months. I'll see the country this way.'

'Once with the circus, always with the circus.'

'Well, you have your Indu.'

'I don't. I hear she's getting engaged to that cricket-playing princeling. I hate all cricketers!'

'You're better-looking.'

'But I'm not a prince. I haven't any money, and I don't play cricket. Well, I played a little at school, but they always made me twelfth man, which meant carrying out the drinks like a waiter. What a stupid game!'

'I agree. Football is better.'

'More manly. But not as glamorous.'

Sitaram pondered a while, and then gave me the benefit of his wisdom.

'To win Indu you must win her mother.'

'And how do I do that? She's a dragon.'

'Well, you must pretend you like dragons.'

I was sitting in the Indiana, having my coffee, when Indu's mother walked in. She was alone. (Indu was probably with her prince, learning to bowl under-arm). I said good morning and asked her if she'd like to join me for a cup of coffee. To my surprise, she assented. Larry Gomes was playing *Love is a Many-Splendoured Thing*, and the

Maharani was just a bit dreamy-eyed and probably a little sloshed too. But she wasn't in any way attractive. Her eyes were baggy (did she drink?) and her skin was coarse (too many skin lotions?) and her chin was developing a dewlap. Would Indu look like her one day?

She drank her coffee and asked me if I would like a drive. On the assumption that she would be driving me to her house, I thanked her and followed her out of the restaurant, while Larry Gomes looked anxiously at me over his spectacles and broke into the *Funeral March*.

Fifteen

Well, it was very nearly my funeral.

Have you ever made love to a dragon—and a scaly one at that? How could a monster like the Maharani have produced a beautiful, tender, vivacious, electrifying girl like Indu? It was like making a succulent dish from a pumpkin, a bitter gourd and a spent cucumber.

The Maharani had denied me the dish, but she was prepared to give me the ingredients.

She drove me to her home in her smart little Sunbeam-Talbot, and no sooner was I settled on her sofa, with a glass of Carew's Gin in my hand, than I found my free hand encased in a fold of crocodile skin—*her* hand!

A shudder ran down my spine. She mistook the shudder for a shiver of excitement, and started playing with the lobe of my ear. My ear got

91

caught between two of her gold bangles and was almost wrenched off as I jerked my head away. Gin was spilt on my trousers, and I put the glass down on a sidetable. As I did so, the Maharani cuddled up to me, and I discovered that the sofa wasn't really large enough for both of us. Also, one was inclined to sink deeper into the upholstery, making a quick escape very difficult.

It had never occured to me that this badly-preserved Christmas pudding could be of an amorous disposition. I had always thought of middle-aged mothers as having gone beyond the pursuit of carnal pleasures. But not this one!

She tried to set me at my ease.

'I'm a child psychologist, you know.'

'But I'm twenty-one.'

'All the better to *treat* you, my dear.'

'Your Highness,' I began.

'Don't Highness me, darling. My pet name is Liz.'

'As in lizard?'

'Cheeky! After Queen Elizabeth.' And she gave me a sharp pinch on the thigh. 'You write poetry, don't you? Recite one of your poems.'

'You need moonlight and roses.'

'I prefer sunshine and cactii.'

'Well, here's a funny one.' I was anxious to please her without succumbing to her blandishments and advances. So I recited my latest limerick.

There was a fat man in Lucknow
Who swallowed six plates of pillau,
When his belly went bust
(As distended, it must)
His buttons rained down upon Mhow.

She clapped her hands and shrieked with delight. 'Buttons, buttons!' And she made a grab for mine. (We weren't using zips in those days.)

I tried to get up from the sofa, but she pulled me down again.

'You deserve a reward,' she said, producing a lump of barley-sugar from a box on the side-table. 'This came all the way from Calcutta. Open your mouth.'

Dutifully I opened my mouth. But instead of popping the sweet in, she planted her lips on mine, large lips like suction pumps, and thrust her long lizard-like tongue down my throat. Her crocodile fingers were all over me, and even if my buttons did not reach Mhow, they must have landed on Mussoorie.

What can you do in such a situation? Not much, really. You just let the more active partner take over—in this case, the rich Maharani of Magador. She certainly knew how to get you worked up. After a hesitant start, all I had to do was imagine that I was another crocodile. I slid into her quivering orifice, and my virginity was at an end.

Afterwards I was rewarded with more barley-sugar and Turkish coffee.

She offered to drop me home, but I said I would walk. Physically I felt great, but I wanted to put my head in order. My thoughts were in whirl. How could I be the Maharani's lover while I was in love with her daughter? Love lyrics for Indu, and limericks for her mother?

'There's no justice anywhere,' I said aloud, in my best William Brown manner. "T'isn't fair.' And then, as Popeye would have said, 'It's disgustipating!'

And as I closed the gate and stepped onto the sidewalk, who should appear but Indu, riding pillion on her cricketing prince's Triumph motorbike. At the sight of him my feelings of guilt evaporated. And looking at Indu, smiling insincerely at me, I began to see points of resemblance between her and her mother. Would she be like the Maharani in twenty years' time? I had never seen her father (the late deceased Maharaja of Magador) but fervently hoped that he had been as goodlooking as his portraits suggested and that Indu had taken after him.

I gave her and her escort a polite bow (part of my grandmother's influence, no doubt) and set off at a dignified pace in the direction of the bazaar. A car would never be mine, but at least my legs wouldn't atrophy from disuse. Hadn't this very cricketing legend suffered from several torn ligaments in the course of his short career? Chasing cricket balls is a certain way to get a hernia, I said to myself, and then turned my thoughts to the composition of a new limerick in honour of the lady who had just tormented me into becoming her lover. There was no Amnesty International in those days; I had to defend myself in my own way. So I composed the following lines:

They called her the Queen of the Nile,
For she walked like a fat crocodile.
But she said, 'You young bugger,
I'll make you my *mugger*,'
And took me to bed with a smile.

Sixteen

We all need one friend in whom to confide—to whom we can confess our misdemeanours, look for sympathy in times of trouble. Sitaram was my only intimate, and he listened with bated breath while I gave him a hair-raising account of my seduction by royalty. But he wasn't sympathetic. His first response was the following succinct remark:

'Congratulations, *ullu ka pattha*.'

'Why the heady compliment?' I asked.

'Because you cannot escape her now. She'll suck you dry.'

'A succubus, forsooth!'

'Don't use fancy language—you know what I mean. When an older woman gets hold of a young man, she doesn't let him go until he's quite useless to her or anyone else! You'd better join the circus with me.'

'And what do I do in the circus? Feed the animals?'

'They need someone for giving massage.'

'I've always fancied myself as a masseur. Whom do I get to massage—the acrobats, the dancing-girls, the trapeze artistes?'

'The elephants. They lie down and you massage their legs. And backsides.'

'I'll stick to the Maharani,' I said. 'Her skin has the same sort of texture, but there's not so much of it.'

'Well, please yourself . . . See, I've brought you a pretty tree. Will you look after it while I'm away?'

It was a red oleander in a pot. It was just coming into flower. We placed it on the balcony beside the rose bush and the geraniums. There were several geraniums now—white, cerise, salmon-pink and bright red—and they were all in flower, making quite a display on the sunny verandah.

'I'll look after them,' I said. 'As long as the landlady doesn't turn me out. The rent is overdue.'

'Don't lend money to your friends. Especially that Swiss fellow. He owes money everywhere—hasn't even paid my parents for two months' washing. One of these days he'll just go away—

and your money with him. There is nothing to keep him here.'

'There is nothing to keep *me* here.'

'This is where you belong, where you grew up. You will always be here.'

It was where I had grown up—my mother's, her parents' home—but I had always been happier with my father, sharing a wartime tent with him on the outskirts of Delhi or Karachi; visiting the ruins of Old Delhi—Humayun's Tomb, the Purana Killa, the Kashmiri Gate; going to the cinema with him to see the beautiful skating legend Sonja Henie in *Sun Valley Serenade*, Nelson Eddy singing *Volga Boatmen* and *Ride, Cossack, Ride* in *Balalaika*, Carmen Miranda swinging her hips *Down Argentine Way*, and Hope and Crosby *On the Road to Zanzibar* or *Morocco* or *Singapore*; rickshaw-rides in Shimla; ice-creams at Davico's; comics—*Film Fun* and *Hotspur* . . . And those colourful postcards he used to send me once a week. At school, the distribution of the post was always something to look forward to.

But I must also have inherited a great deal of my mother's sensuality, her unconventional attitude to life, her stubborn insistence on doing things that respectable people did not approve of ... Traits that she probably got from her father, a convivial character, who mingled with all and shocked not a few.

I'm sure my mother was quite a handful for my poor father, bookish and intellectual, who did so want her to be a 'lady'. But this was something that went against her nature. She liked to drink and swear a bit. The ladies of the Dehra Benevolent Society did not approve. Nor did they approve of my mother going to church without a hat! This was considered the height of irreverence in those days. There were remonstrances and anguished letters of protest from other (always female) members of the Congregation.

As a result, my mother stopped going to church, and I never picked up the habit. Her sisters, with the exception of the eldest, Enid, were conventional types who found and kept conventional husbands. Aunt Enid, though married to a doctor, distributed her favours on a first-come, first-served basis; she wasn't particular about the cut of your trousers as long as there was something in them. She liked having a good time, and in those war years there was no shortage of Allied troops prepared to make her their mascot. She had a daughter, Sally, who was my age and a bit of a tomboy. Sally and I wrestled in Granny's flowerbeds and took a spirited interest in each other's anatomy. We were only six or seven, and it was all innocent play—or arrested foreplay, I suppose. We sucked each other's lollipops, and this gave us as great a thrill as anything else we did.

Growing up in fairly unfettered fashion, I was quite at ease with Sitaram, another free soul. I was not so sure about the Maharani, although I suspect Aunt Enid would have approved of her. Would she pursue me with relentless abandon, as Sitaram feared, or would she already be looking for other conquests? If she was anything like Aunt E, it would be the latter.

Seventeen

The circus tents were being dismantled and the parade-ground was comparatively silent again. Some boys kicked a football around. Others flew kites. The monsoon season is kite-flying time, for it's not too windy, and the moist aircurrents are just right for keeping a kite aloft.

In the old part of the Dhamawalla bazaar, there used to be a kite-shop (it was still there five years ago, when I revisited the area), and, taking a circuitous way home, I stopped at the shop and bought a large pink kite. I thought Sitaram would enjoy flying it from the rooftop when he wasn't dancing in the rain. But when I got home, I found he had gone. His parents told me he had left in a hurry, as most of the circus people had taken the afternoon train to Amritsar. He had taken his clothes and a cracked bathroom mirror,

101

nothing else, and yet the flat seemed strangely empty and forlorn without him. The plants on the balcony were poignant reminders of his presence.

I thought of giving the kite to my landlady's son, but I knew him for a destructive brat who'd put his fist through it at the first opportunity, so I hung it on a nail on the bedroom wall, and thought it looked rather splendid there, better than a Picasso although perhaps not in the same class as one of Jai Shankar's angels.

As I stood back, admiring it, there was a loud knocking at my door (as in the knocking at the gate in Macbeth, portending deeds of darkness) and I turned to open it, wondering why I had bothered to close it in the first place (I seldom did), when something about the knocking—its tone, its texture—made me hesitate.

There are knocks of all kinds—hesitant knocks, confident knocks, friendly knocks, good-news knocks, bad-news knocks, tax-collector's knocks (exultant, these!), policemen's knocks (peremptory, business-like), drunkard's knocks (slow and deliberate), the landlady's knock (you could tell she owned the place) and children's knocks (loud thumps halfway down the door).

I had come to recognize different kinds of knocks, but this one, was unfamiliar. It was a possessive kind of knock, gloating, sensual, bold and arrogant. I stood a chair on a table, then balanced myself on the chair and peered down through the half-open skylight.

It was Indu's mother. Her perfume nearly knocked me off the chair. Her bosom heaved with passion and expectancy, her eyes glinted like a hyaena's and her crocodile hands were encased in white gloves!

I withdrew quietly and tiptoed back across the room and out on the balcony. On the next balcony, my neighbour's maidservant was hanging out some washing.

'For God's sake,' I told her. 'That woman out front, banging on my door. Go and tell her I'm not at home!'

'Who is she?'

'A *rakshasni*, if you want to know.'

'Then I'm not going near her!'

'All right, can you let me out through your flat? Is there anyone at home?'

'No, but come quickly. Can you climb over the partition?'

The partition did not look as if it would take

my weight, so I climbed over the balcony wall and, clinging to it, moved slowly along the ledge till I got to my neighbour's balcony. The maidservant helped me over. Such nice hands she had! How could a working girl have such lovely hands while a lady of royal lineage had crocodile-skin hands? It was the Law of Compensation, I suppose; Mother Nature looking after her own.

'What's your name?' I whispered, as she led me through her employer's flat and out to the back stairs.

'Radha,' she said, her smile lighting up the gloom.

'Rather you than that rakshasni outside!' I gave her hand a squeeze and said, 'I'll see you again,' then took off down the stairs as though a swarm of bees was after me.

My landlady's son's bicycle was standing in the verandah. I decided to borrow it for a couple of hours.

I rode vigorously until I was out of the town, and then I took a narrow unmetalled road through the sal forest on the Hardwar road. I thought I would be safe there, but it wasn't long before I heard the menacing purr of the Maharani's Sunbeam-Talbot. Looking over my shoulder, I saw it bumping along in a cloud of dust. It was like a chase-scene in a Hitchcock film, and I was Cary Grant about to be machinegunned from a low-flying aircraft. I saw another narrow trail to the right, and swerved off the road, only to find myself parting company with the bicycle and somersaulting into some lantana bushes. There was a screech of brakes, a car door shot open and the rich Maharani of Magador was bounding towards me like a man-eating tigress.

'Jim Corbett, where are you?' I called feebly.

'He's in Kenya, you fool,' said the tigress, as she engulfed me and swallowed me whole.

Eighteen

A change of air was needed. What with the attentions of the Maharani, the borrowings of William, the loss of Indu and the absence of Sitaram, I wasn't doing much writing. My bank balance was very low. I had also developed a throat infection, probably as a result of having that rasping lizard's tongue slide down my throat. Anyone else would have bitten it off!

There was the sum of two hundred and seventy rupees in the bank. Always prudent, I withdrew two hundred and fifty and left twenty rupees for my last supper. Then I packed a bag, and left my keys with the landlady with the entreaty that she tell no one in Dehra of my whereabouts and took the bus to Rishikesh.

Rishikesh was then little more than a village, scattered along the banks of the Ganga where it cut through the foothills. There were a few ashrams and temples, a tiny bazaar and a police outpost. The saffron-robed sadhus and ascetics outnumbered the rest of the population.

There had been a break in the rains, and I spent a night sleeping on the sands sloping down to the river. The next night it did rain, and I moved to a bench on the small railway platform. I could have stayed in one of the two ashrams, but I had no pretensions to religion of any kind, and was not inclined to become an acolyte to some holy man. Kim had his Lama, the braying Beatles had their Master and others have had their gurus and godmen, but I have always been stubborn and thick-headed enough to want to remain my own man—just myself, warts and all, singing my own song. Nobody's *chela*, nobody's camp-follower.

Let nature reign, let freedom sing! . . .

And, so, on the third morning of my voluntary exile from the fleshpots of Dehra, I strode up river, taking a well-worn path which led to the shrines in the higher mountains. I was not seeking salvation or enlightenment; I wished merely to come to terms with myself and my situation.

Should I stay on in Dehra, or should I strike

out for richer pastures—Delhi or Bombay perhaps?
Or should I return to London and my desk in the
Thomas Cook office? Oh, for the life of a clerk!
Or I could give English tuitions, I supposed.
Except that everyone seemed to know English.
What about French? I'd picked up a French patois
in the Channel Islands. It wasn't the real thing,
but who would know the difference?

I practised a few lines, reciting aloud to
myself:

Jeune femme au rendezvous.
(Waiting for her lover.)
Oh, Oui! Il va venir
(Oh, yes, he is coming!)
Enfin je le verrai!
(Finally I shall see him!)
Pourquoi je attends?
(What am I waiting for?)

Roll up, folks. Learn how to make love in French!
I could see my flat overflowing with students from
all over Dehra and beyond. But how was I to keep
the Maharani from attending?

The future looked rather empty as I trudged
forlornly up the mountain trail. What I really
needed just then was a good companion—someone

to confide in, someone with whom to share life's little problems. No wonder people get married! An admirable institution, marriage. But who'd marry an indigent writer, with twenty rupees in the bank and no prospects in a land where English was on the way out. (I was not to know that English would be 'in' again, thirty years later.) No self-respecting girl really wants to share the proverbial attic with a down-and-out writer; least of all the princess Indu from Magador. I was pretty sure her mother would let me stay in the garage—but for how long? She was the sort who tired pretty quickly of her playthings.

I should have taken my cricket more seriously, I told myself. Must dress better. Put on the old school tie.

This depressing thought in mind, I found myself standing on the middle of a small wooden bridge that crossed one of the swift mountain streams that fed the great river. No, I wasn't thinking of hurling myself on the rocks below. The thought would have terrified me! I'm the sort who clings to life no matter how strong the temptation is to leave it. But absent-mindedly I leant against the wooden railing of the bridge. The wood was rotten and gave way immediately.

I fell some thirty feet, fortunately into the middle of the stream where the water was fairly deep. I did not strike any rocks. But the current was swift and carried me along with it. I could swim a little (thank God for those two years in the Channel Islands), and as I'd lost my chappals in my fall, I swam and drifted with the current, even though my clothes were an encumbrance. The breast-stroke seemed the best in those turbulent waters, but ahead I saw a greater turbulence and knew I was approaching rapids and, possibly, a waterfall. That would have spelt the end of a promising young writer.

So I tried desperately to reach the river bank on my right. I got my hands on a smooth rock but was pulled away by the current. Then I clutched at the branch of a dead tree that had fallen into the stream. I held fast; but I did not have the strength to pull myself out of the water.

Looking up I saw my father standing on the grassy bank. He was smiling at me in the way he had done that lazy afternoon at the canal. Was he beckoning to me to join him in the next world, or urging me to make a bid to continue for a while in this one?

I made a special effort—yes, I was a

stouthearted boy—heaved myself out of the water
and climbed along the waterlogged tree-trunk
until I sank into ferns and soft grass.

I looked up again, but the vision had gone.
The air was scented with wild roses and magnolia.

You may break, you may shatter
  the vase if you will,
But the scent of the roses will linger
  there still.

Nineteen

Back to sleepy Dehra, somnolent in the hot afternoon sun and humid from the recent rain. Dragonflies hovered over the canals. Mosquitoes bred in still waters, multiplying their own species and putting a brake on ours. Someone at the bus stand told me that the Maharani was down with malaria; as a result I walked through the bazaar with a spring in my step, even though my cheap new chappals were cutting into the flesh between my toes. Underfoot, the neem-pods gave out their refreshing though pungent odour. This was home, even though it did not offer fame or riches.

As I approached Astley Hall, I saw a kite flying from the roof of my flat. The landlady's son had probably got hold of it. It darted about, pirouetted, made extravagant nose-dives, recovered and went through teasing little acrobatic sallies, as though it had a life of its own. A pink kite against a turquoise-blue sky.

It was definitely my kite. How dare my landlady presume I had no need for it! I hurried to the stairs, stepping into cowdung as I went and consoling myself with the thought that stepping into fresh cow-dung was considered lucky, at least according to Sitaram's mother.

And perhaps it was, because, as I took the narrow stairway to the flat roof, who should I find up there but Sitaram himself, flying my kite without a care in the world.

When he saw me, he tied the kite-string to a chimney-stack and ran up and gave me a tight hug and bit me on the cheek.

'Why aren't you with the circus?' I asked.

'Left the circus,' he said, and we sat down on the parapet and exchanged news.

'What made you leave so suddenly? You were ready to follow those circus-girls wherever they went.'

'They are all in Ambala. There's a big parade-ground there. But it was too hot. Much hotter than Dehra.'

'Is that why you left—because of the heat?'

'Well, there was also this tiger that escaped.'

'But it escaped in Dehra! Don't tell me it returned to the circus?'

'No, no! This was the other tiger. It got out of its cage, somehow.'

'Not again! Did *you* have anything to do with it?'

'Of course not. I hadn't been near it since early that morning.'

'Someone must have left the cage open. Or failed to close it properly.'

'Must have been Mr Victor, the ringmaster. Anyway, when he tried to drive it back into the cage, it sprang on him and took his arm off. He's in hospital.'

'And the tiger?'

'It ran into the sugarcane fields. No one saw it again.'

'So the circus has lost two tigers and the ringmaster his arm. Has the lion escaped too, since you've been there?'

'No, the lion's too old. Besides, it's deeply in love with the lady-wrestler.'

'I thought that was the dwarf.'

'They both love her.'

I gave up. I had a sneaking suspicion that he'd had something to do with the escape of the tiger, but he managed to convince me that he'd come back (a) because of the heat, and (b) because he missed me. In that order. Had it been the other way round, I wouldn't have believed him.

I collected my keys from the landlady (Sitaram had got into the flat through the skylight, anxious to find clues to my whereabouts), and she gave me a couple of letters. One of them contained a cheque from the *Weekly*, with a note from its editor, C.R. Mandy, saying he would be happy to serialize my novel, *The Room on the Roof*. The cheque was for seven hundred rupees.

'We're rich!' I shouted, showing Sitaram the cheque. 'Well, for two or three months, at least . . . See, I told you I'd be a successful writer some day!'

'Will there be more cheques?'

'As long as I keep writing.'

'Then sit down and write.' He pulled a chair up for me and forced me to sit in front of my desk.

'Not now, you ass. I'll start tomorrow.'

'No, *today*!'

And so, to make him happy, I wrote a new limerick:

There was a young fellow called Ram
Who set up a frantic alarm,

For he'd let loose a tiger,
Two bears and a liger,
Who bit off the ringmaster's arm.

'What's a liger?'
'A cross between a lion and a lady-wrestler.'
'Write more about me.'
'Tomorrow. Now let's go out and celebrate.'

We went to one of the sweetshops near the bazaar and ate jalebis. Jai Shankar found us there and we ate more jalebis.

Then, walking down Rajpur Road, we met William Matheson, who said he was badly in need of a drink. So we took him to the Royal Cafe, where we found Suresh Mathur expounding on the fourth dimension. There were a great many drinks, and everyone got drunk. Suresh Mathur so forgot himself that he signed the chit for the drinks.

It was late evening when we rolled into the Indiana for dinner. Larry Gomes played *Roll Out the Barrel* and joined us for a beer.

I couldn't write the next day because I had a terrible hangover. But I started again the following day, and I have been writing ever since.

Epilogue

The friendly reader knows that I have continued scribbling away for forty years, but he (or she) might well be interested in knowing what happened to the other nuts described in the foregoing pages.

Unlike her mother, Indu grew old quite gracefully. She did not marry the Purkazi prince, as the Maharani had hoped; and this was just as well, for his nose was permanently disfigured by a bump-ball hurled at him by a West Indies paceman. He retired shortly afterward and became a sports journalist known for his bitter diatribes against his fellow cricketers and fast bowlers in particular. Indu married a hotelier in Mauritius where she spends most of her time.

The Maharani of Magador went quite potty in her declining years, took to the bottle and became convinced that she'd been Mae West in a previous incarnation. Whenever she saw a good-looking man approaching, she welcomed him with the line, 'Is that a gun in your pocket, or are you just happy to see me?'

I met her a few months before she died. She was sitting at the bar of a well-know club in New Delhi, and when I greeted her deferentially, she looked me up and down speculatively and said, 'You're that writer chap, Bunskin Ronde, aren't you? Tried to seduce me when I was a girl!'

William Matheson returned to Switzerland, where he inherited a fortune from his father and lived the good life for a number of years; but he never returned the money he'd borrowed from me.

Suresh Mathur went to practise law in the neighbouring hill station of Mussoorie, a resort that at close quarters looked as though it had been hammered out of old biscuit-tins. It is prettier at night when darkness hides the scars on its cardboard hillsides. Suresh had one too many Vodka Marys, and finally entered the fourth dimension.

Jai Shankar went to Oxford, where he painted a mural for his college dining-room. Apparently the boat-crew did not like it and dumped him in the Thames near Tilbury. He gave up art when one of his models sued him for exhibiting a painting in which he had shown her with three breasts. He now lives in Paris and writes poems in French.

And what of dear Sitaram?

No, he did not enter his father's profession. He remained with me for another year, and then, at the age of eighteen, decided to try his luck in Mumbai, then Bombay. He went to work for a well-known actress, who liked his winning ways and got him a small part in one of her films. After that, he went from strength to strength and by the time he was in his thirties he was one of the most popular stars of the Indian screen. He wrote to me a couple of times and asked me to come and stay with him; but I felt shy of his success and stayed away. The bright lights, whether in the circus or on the film-sets, were not for me. The writer's art is a lonely one.

Of course Sitaram became famous under another, assumed name, and I am sure, dear reader, that you would like to know his identity. But I have promised to keep it a secret, and so we must leave it at that. But I'll give you a few clues:

he doesn't sing, though he dances; he can't act but he has a sexy smile; and although the hair on his head is jet-black, the hair on his torso is now quite grey. But most of them are a bit like that, aren't they?